An Outcast but prodigious University of British Columbia senior struggles to master blossoming supernatural talents. As she questions what she knows about the afterlife, she discovers an underground community of kindred people. With their help to hone her curious array of skills, she solves a centuries-old murder by communing with the dead.

Warrior's Dawn
Copyright © 2019 Ella Harrison
ISBN: 978-1-4874-1592-1
Cover art by Martine Jardin

Published by eXtasy Books Inc or
Devine Destinies, an imprint of eXtasy Books Inc

Look for us online at:
www.eXtasybooks.com or www.devinedestinies.com

Warrior's Dawn
Warrior Prequel

By

Ella Harrison

DEDICATION

I would like to thank both strangers and family alike that believed in me, all the people who never said you can't do this. I would especially like to thank my husband for his never-ending service and sacrifice to me, our family, and everyone else.

CHAPTER ONE: AWAKENING

Ada shifted anxiously in her seat as a thick, gingery ringlet of her hair escaped the tight French braid next to her temple. Rays of lingering afternoon sunlight caught in the coil of hair, reating a ring of golden fire that bounced out of the corner of her eye with every movement. It was the first day of her senior year in college, and Ada did not expect a warm welcome — having always been dubbed the odd one out. Sure enough, today was no different.

Thinking back to previous years of school when she was often the butt of jokes and prank fodder, she knew it would be another year of failing to make friends. Her anxiety began to make her face flush. In an effort to deal with the nervous energy, she shuffled her notebooks and binders around in her bag again. As she rummaged through her books, time slowed down. The metal leg of her chair felt like ice as her hand brushed against it. She heard her thick braid rustle against her black jogging suit as it fell forward. Then she felt it. Someone was looking at her. She physically felt someone's eyes boring into her back.

Here it comes. A bad joke from a classmate and another over-sensitive-psycho moment from me, complete with a slow-mo effect. Because, you know, everyone has one of those moments on the first day of class!

Her mind was quick to condemn these moments after years of bizarre time slow occurrences. She still hadn't learned why they happened, what they meant, or how they could be useful — if she could control them. They had plagued her childhood, along with other unusual things including strange dreams and premonitions.

Ada's grandmother Della attributed it to the loss of her parents when she was a small girl. However, she had met other orphaned children in her group grief counseling sessions, and no one mentioned anything of the sort happening to them.

Movement caught her eye, and she turned her head in time to catch the professor closing the classroom door about ten feet from her desk. He stopped dead in his tracks with his hand still on the doorknob, staring directly into her eyes. His gaze lasted a little too long. She broke eye contact with him, straightened her back, and shifted her gaze to the front of the room. It seemed like he felt that time had slowed for her. His eyes bore into hers. She felt the heat rise in her cheeks. *Maybe it was just my hair gleaming in the sunlight. It does take people off guard.* Rationalizing the moment did little to shake the feeling that something was off about her professor.

She felt time slow further to a snail's pace. As her braid swung back into place, it sounded and felt like bristling fields of wheat swaying in the wind. She felt the heat rising again in her cheeks. The sun felt like a laser beam behind her, and a trickle of sweat—induced by her rapidly rising panic—slid down the small of her back. She heard the hand on the clock above the whiteboard tick with deafening finality. She closed her eyes, took a deep breath and squared her shoulders.

Stare straight ahead, Ada, like a good pupil. Don't let on that you're the psycho who thinks she can hear her own hair. Chin up.

She exhaled, blowing a few stray curls out of her face. Just at that moment she felt an unexpectedly warm hand on her shoulder, and a calming sensation instantly washed over her brittle nerves. She turned and met the professor's piercing brown eyes.

At close range, she realized his eyes were a shade too light, a warm caramel as opposed to the mahogany brown she expected. They were round and soulful. They seemed to speak without a voice. His hair was wiry, cut short, and was salt-and-pepper colored. His face was creased with wisdom. She felt like she knew him already, which was bizarre because she'd never taken any of his classes.

Ada was still a little taken aback by his soul-piercing gaze, so she looked away from him and down at her notepad. After he placed his hand on her shoulder, time began to march forward again, and she felt relief wash over her fragile psyche. The professor addressed the class, with his hand still on her shoulder.

"Let young Miss Ada here be our exemplar and Luminary in class. She has already ordered and reordered her color-coded notebooks three times and rearranged her pencils according to size."

The professor seemed to be jittery and nervous as he finished speaking. *What would he have to be nervous about? I'm the one having a mental breakdown over the sound of my own hair!*

Raucous, booming laughter escaped the smallish man beside her as the entire class turned around to gawk at her. She felt thirty pairs of judging eyes on her and her unruly hair, which was now beginning to escape the tight braid in earnest. Her cheeks flushed from pink to crimson. *Don't cry. Don't cry. Don't cry.* The professor's voice boomed again, distracting her from the hot tears she felt welling up in her round brown eyes.

"If you were to look in my desk, it looks like an angry toddler rifled through the whole thing, and he brought his best toddler buddy to have a second go at it."

Laughter broke out slowly, and the students began to loosen up. He bent over and looked into Ada's eyes one more time for good measure. He patted her shoulder before finally letting go, then began walking to the whiteboard.

Ada noticed that he moved with the grace of a much younger man. His walk was peculiarly silent, and she felt her eyes shift down to look at his shoes. She recognized the pebbly grain of bison leather on his loafers. They were heavily worn and beginning to fray—the mark of a man who lived frugally. He reached the front of the room and turned to face the students with a flourish of his hand which Ada would almost describe as giddy—although the giddiness was tempered by wisdom.

"My name is Mathias, and I will be your professor and your pedagogue. Although I hold dual doctorates in both theology and philosophy from Harvard University, do understand that I am your humble guide and do not expect to be addressed as Dr. Mathias."

Another definitively giddy laugh erupted from *Dr. Mathias*. Several students chimed in as well, enjoying their professor's humor. Ordinarily undergraduate professors were stuffy, with lofty opinions and expectations. Many were known for correcting students when they failed to address them as *doctor*.

"I have been teaching here at the University of British Columbia for thirty years, and yes it's true I taught World Religion to our Provost many moons ago. This course is Religion, Myths and the Afterlife, coded HIST 407.

"I prefer a cell phone and laptop-free classroom. If it's an emergency and you must check your phone, please do so outside, during the break if possible.

"And yes, I am the teacher who does off-site lectures at Hatley and Craigdarroch Castles. We will also have lectures at other rumored haunted historic sites around the area. This course is, after all, a study of the afterlife and religion."

He turned to the whiteboard and began writing in flowing, elegant strokes. "We will write a single research paper this semester, and this paper will serve as your midterm and final exam. The thesis is due along with a rough outline of the final paper at midterm. You will each be assigned a partner. I'll email all of you personally and let you know who it is and their contact information.

"We meet twice a week from two to five, Tuesdays and Fridays. Tuesdays we are always here. Once a week we will have offsite lectures, typically on Fridays in a location known to have significant paranormal or unexplained activity. The full list of locations is in the class syllabus."

His voice began to drone in Ada's ears and she mentally unplugged for a moment from the classroom. She was looking forward to the course, but she was also feeling overwhelmed. Her jogging suit was zipped up to her chin and began to feel like a straitjacket. A trickle of sweat began to pool between her breasts. A small river slid down the small of her back. She unzipped it and gazed out the window across the campus.

Fall was setting in, and the leaves were beginning their transformation, but some days were still warm. The temperature would drop in the evenings to an uncomfortable chill.

The crisp air of fall suited her stormy emotions and almost soothed her turbulent mind. Some days she felt bombarded, with so many odd things happening. Today was no exception, and she truly began to wonder if her idiosyncrasies might land her in *crazy-cat-lady-who-doesn't-leave-the-house* territory someday.

The window was open, and the fresh fall air wafted over her damp skin. She tuned back to Mathias at that moment, realizing she might be missing something. A deep crimson oak leaf wafted into the classroom, whirling and twirling in the cool air.

Chris was sitting immediately to Ada's right and saw the leaf whirl through the open window and land with seeming intention into her hair. It looked like Mother Nature had crowned her queen with an oak leaf as the late afternoon sun shined on her thick hair, making it erupt in a thousand shades of chocolate and crimson.

He noticed how tense her body was, with her gaze oddly fixated on the professor. She was coiled too tightly, like an overwound spring. Her arms were on top of her desk, hands palm down on either side of her notebook, round eyes transfixed ahead. Chris reveled in the curious shade of her eye color that was remarkably similar to his own. He closed his eyes for a moment and inhaled. As he closed his eyes, time slowed for him. He focused on Ada and her scent. The air was heavy with her fear, along with the smell of rose oil and a twinge of her annoyance. Just as he was *a little too perfect,* so was she.

He noticed her breasts were too large for a delicate frame, her waist too small, and her hips too large for everything else. Her eyes appeared to be a little too round and her hair just a bit too perfect. Her efforts to disguise it failed as she attempted to tame it with the braid. He could smell her sweat as it trickled between her breasts. *She's just trying to blend in. Like me.*

The virile young man with his burnished mahogany skin and model perfect body exhaled deeply. He attempted to steal another glance at his ethereal classmate as she shifted in her seat and tilted her head down, gripping a strange silver filigreed pen like it was a weapon. She scratched a few things down on the notepad. Instinctively, he reached to pluck the leaf from her braid.

Ada's eyes widened as she realized a large perfectly manicured hand was in her personal space. As she whipped her head around to see what was going on, she caught sight of his hand settling over something behind her head.

The next thing she knew, he was untangling a large oak leaf from her rebellious hair. The leaf seemed to have adhered to her head, as if Mother Nature was not ready to relinquish the crown to a less worthy candidate.

Their eyes met, and Ada's breath caught as she locked gazes with the most beautiful male creature she'd ever seen. He looked to be about two hundred and sixty pounds and six feet of the quintessential chocolate Ken doll. His face was perfect, except for his eyes. Like those of both herself and Mathias, his eyes were a slightly unnerving shade of pale brown — warm but unusual, to say the least.

He was wearing a plain white t-shirt and gray jogging pants. His broad shoulders and slim waist were accentuated by the flimsy material of his jogging suit. Muscles rippled beneath the thin fabric as he shifted in his seat.

She was intrigued by his pale brown eyes, and an anxious smile inched across her face. He smiled back at her, his full lips and white teeth glinting in the sunlight with bizarre perfection, just like hers.

The tank top under her jacket was doing a lousy job of containing her breasts, and she felt them begin to bust out of the opening. *Great, now he probably thinks I am some kind of salacious harlot.*

Mathias's booming voice broke into Ada's mind. It roughly snapped her out of her inquisitive peeping on the mahogany-hued god next to her. *How fortuitous. At least there will be nice scenery during this class.*

"This Friday our off-site lecture will be at The Vogue Theatre. Please familiarize yourself with its storied history, including the alleged hauntings.

"Read chapters one through nine and outline the main theories the text describes to date regarding hauntings and the afterlife. Everyone is expected to speak in class, FYI, so please come armed with some scholarly literature regarding hauntings, or firsthand accounts of your own."

She watched as he sat gingerly on the edge of his desk with cat-like precision. He folded his arms in front of him before continuing.

"Please also check the list of partner pairings in the syllabus and get in touch with each other. My recommendation is that you determine a method of communication that works for both of you right off the bat. We have a student study group that meets every Wednesday around five at Boho Luna, that kitschy new café just off campus."

His eyes surveyed the room carefully. It looked like he was looking for something or someone. *He's such a strange one. It's a class full of students. What could he possibly be combing over the group for?*

"It's in that old frat house where the news did a story on suicide clustering a few years ago. The frat shut it down shortly after and sold the building. A great spot to gather, given the spirit of our coursework. Pun intended."

A devious but nervous laugh escaped his lips despite his visible efforts to contain it.

"I look forward to seeing you on Friday. For now, I must bid you adieu."

Mathias peculiarly clicked the back of his heels together at that point and began to bow. Ada did a double take to make sure she wasn't daydreaming. Bizarre daydreams had plagued her for years, and she wasn't totally sure at first this wasn't another episode.

She tilted her head to the side as her professor completed a very deep bow, then turned around dramatically, grabbed his satchel, and walked out of the room, slamming the door behind him. The entire class jumped out of their seats when the door slammed into its frame. *Well, everyone saw that. I am not crazy.* Her eyes widened and then narrowed in skepticism at what she'd just witnessed.

The students began to rumble amongst themselves as they started packing up. She felt the atmosphere in the room develop a somewhat disconcerted response to the professor's slightly-off-kilter exit. Suddenly feeling like there was a shortage of oxygen, she stood up and hurriedly started packing her things. The other students were talking amongst themselves about how bohemian Mathias seemed and how unusual this class would be for the rest of the semester. It looked to be a refreshing break from writing redundant term papers and the laborious time squandering calculus class. She enjoyed their small talk, even though she felt left out. She always seemed to be on the outside looking in, and she had made peace with that long ago. She still enjoyed being near other people, even if it meant she wasn't part of their social circles.

She wondered where her joy had gone. The students around her were basking in the dewy vibrancy of their youth. As naïve as they were, they still recognized they were young, and life was before them to live. All *her* life she'd felt wisdom beyond her years, accompanied by an inexplicable burden that felt like the weight of the world on her shoulders. She could not put her finger on what that burden was or where it came from, and that made it all the more frustrating. *What I would give to experience their joie de vivre.*

Ada forced time to slow for her and watched them for a moment. She couldn't always slow down time at will, but if she concentrated, she could control the ability for a short burst. Her things were packed and ready to go. She regarded them from her seat at the back of the room. When things were slower, it was so much easier to figure them all out. Having long been the odd man out, she had developed an appreciation for people watching.

She watched a girl in the front row flip her long blonde hair over her shoulder and smile vivaciously at the hot but meatheaded quarterback jock beside her. It was common knowledge that he was being courted by more than one team with the NFL. The girls flocked to him, all vying for a chance to sink their claws in before he went pro and their chances would slip away. The blonde was so busy tossing her hair and trying to look perky she failed to notice that meathead was also ogling the shorter-haired brunette behind her. Meanwhile the brunette crossed and uncrossed her legs, her short skirt leaving nothing to the imagination. The raven-haired girl turned her head this way and that as she scribbled something down on a gum wrapper.

Like a chocolate Labrador cocking its head at a strange sound. Ada thought, stifling a giggle.

The brunette got up, slinging her backpack over one shoulder. She snapped her gum and clicked across the floor in her sparkly flip flops as she dropped the gum wrapper on the jock's desk. He was a bit puzzled by the gift and looked up just in time to get a full view of the brunette's barely covered posterior. The jock was so occupied by her ass he never even looked her in the eye when she tried to explain what the gum wrapper contained. Just at that moment the other girl tossed her silky blonde hair over her other shoulder and he forgot about the gum wrapper and the short skirt — just like that. It was like waving a piece of steak in front of a hound dog. *Well, maybe an ass hound.*

Ada shook off the deep thoughts and snapped herself back into normal time. She grabbed her backpack and slung it over her back, careful to adjust the straps on her small shoulders. The bag seemed to accentuate her voluptuous bust by pulling her shoulders back. She felt many eyes pouring over her as she prepared to leave.

A warm cup of spiced tea was calling her name at her city apartment. Then and there, she realized as overwhelming as life could be, she did take joy in many things. A hot bath, a cup of tea, and some research about the hauntings at The Vogue sounded fun. She was also curious about who her partner would be for the course, since it could make or break the fun.

What if I am assigned to meathead? I'll do all the work while he stares deep into my cleavage. What a boob. With that thought a scowl broke out across her face. *Please say it's not the jock.*

Chris was gathering his things as well and noticed the whole exchange with the jock, including the oblivious blonde and the brunette. He'd known the jock for a while, and Kevin was definitely simple-minded. The women clamoring around him stupefied him. They were horrid creatures, truly not interested in much beyond their next manicure or funding their handbag shopping habits. It was a shallow and empty way to live. He lowered his head and whispered in his new friend's ear.

Ava's chiseled seatmate's low rough voice sent a little shiver down her back. She didn't fully understand her feelings toward him. It wasn't quite a sexual attraction, but something else, something familiar. She couldn't put her finger on it. It was like a sense of déjà vu, only deeper.

"Wow, what a meathead. I hope he's not my partner. But the blonde is kind of hot, though in an unimaginative sort of way. If she was my partner, I could have my way with her *and* my own spin on the paper. There'd be no serious drama or thought required, as long as I met her criteria for short-term arm candy . . .and of course as long as I did all the heavy lifting on the term paper."

Deep and dark laughter bubbled up out of the depths of his mind at his own joke—sometimes his dry sense of humor took even him by surprise. He looked at his bewitching classmate. She still looked inexplicably tense, and he thought she could use a laugh. Anything with a pulse in the room could see meathead, blondie, and brunette for what they were—

except them, of course. They were clueless.

At the word *meathead* her eyes widened, since that was the name she had silently used for the buffoon up front. Did her new classmate have some sort of special talent like she did? Did he, too, know a person inside and out as soon as he met them?

She felt her strange senses were all over the place these days, and they seemed more uncontrollable than ever. It was making her jittery, to say the least. She had no one to talk to, no one to ask about what was happening to her. Her parents had disappeared under clouded circumstances, and no bodies were ever found. She thought back to something her grandmother always said. *You're just like your mother . . . always having odd dreams.*

With no one to share her experiences with, Ada had always felt isolated. Her grandmother was her family, but she wasn't remotely like Ada, and she didn't really grasp what was going on in her life. She had a deep seated feeling her classmate was different. Maybe he was even like her. She smiled at him tentatively.

He looked deeply into her eyes for a second too long, making her begin to feel uncomfortable before he broke the awkward silence. Smiling, he cleared his throat self-consciously."This should be a fun class. I've been looking forward to the varying venues for the lectures."

Well, that *was a strangely mundane comment after his staring. Why do I continue to feel like I know this guy?* Feeling over peopled, she finished gathering her things hurriedly, anxious for a warm cup of tea. She smiled at him broadly in an effort to hide how weird she felt about everything that had transpired in the last hour. With a frozen smile plastered on her face she responded to him with equally mundane commentary. "I totally agree. It seems like a great way to experience the supposedly haunted parts of the city. At any rate, it beats a day of studying calculus or World History."

His backpack completed packed, he stood before her with his hands on his hips, his body language signaling that he was ready to leave. "Yeah, it sure does. That's partially why I signed up for the class."

Taking the hint and eager to get home as well, she rushed to end the conversation. Still unsure of what to make of him, she just wanted to get home to regroup. "Well, I've got to get home, lots of homework to do, and hair to wash. Hope to see you at Boho?" she inquired curiously, then studied his reaction as she began walking towards the door.

"Nice! Dirty hair, huh? Sounds like someone has had enough peopling for the day. I get it. I'm Chris, by the way. See you at Boho, for sure. We can comment on the adventures of meathead."

He smiled at her with genuine sincerity and a touch of trepidation, unsure of what to make of his new-found friend. He thought her vulnerability was endearing. He finished packing up, their gazes connecting once more as she made a hasty retreat. After class he headed home in a buoyant mood. He was very curious about this girl. She made him feel less alone, for some reason. He couldn't quite put his finger on it, but there was something familiar about her. *Is familiar the right word?* He tapped a finger against his lips, perplexed. *Weird Déjà vu?*

CHAPTER TWO: CHANGES

A da was anxious for a hot cup of tea so she could process the day. She walked down the darkened halls, zipping her sweatshirt modestly as she passed rambunctious college kids. Soon she was outside in the crisp air headed to her car. An image of a cuddle with her plump tabby cat Mr. Jiggles while doing some homework popped into her mind as she clicked the remote for her car. She slid in the seat and inhaled the new car smell, letting it wash over her. In some ways the solitude of her car felt like a sanctuary, and today was no different. The engine purred to life and soft jazz played. The engine hummed along, and the masterfully engineered suspension in the car made bumps and potholes feel almost nonexistent.

She felt thankful for the trust fund left to her by her parents, as it afforded her fine things such as her sedan. She yawned and let her mind wander a bit. She was mystified about meeting Chris, and she was also floored by Mathias' unusual mannerisms. She felt some *joie de vivre* return as her interest was piqued regarding the class and meeting Chris. *Everyone needs someone. Even if it's not romantic, everyone needs to connect with someone else on a fundamental level.*

She pulled up at her kitschy apartment building full of character and charm. It was an aging 200-year-old brick building renovated with chef's kitchens, beautiful baths, and floors that had been sanded and sealed. Much of the character remained inside, and she loved the exposed brick and beaten up plank floors. The building had been many things, including a brothel at one point. Its storied history hadn't bothered her a bit. Love filled her heart as she thought of her second-floor space, her patio, and how close it was to the university and the city. She hardly heard from her neighbor next door. As a doctor at the local hospital, he seemed to be absorbed by his work and little else. The bottom floor was taken up completely by a retired teacher whose husband had passed away some years before.

The main entry was still large and grand, as it must have been when the space was a brothel. The front door was carved mahogany with a massive panel of stained glass featuring a peacock and a pea hen with their necks curved in the shape of a heart and beaks touching. The peacocks' beautiful plumage fanned around below them, catching the light with dancing sprays of turquoise, emerald, and ochre. Hints of red caught in the late afternoon sun and cast a kaleidoscope of color on the polished warm-hued wooden floors. An ornate staircase with a peacock carved into the banister curved its way up to the second floor. The entryway was vaulted all the way to the third floor, with a glass-paned cupola at the center. She was unsure of what was up on the third floor as no one lived up there and she'd never ventured that far up.

To the left of the entry door stood a large brass set of mailboxes on a pedestal, with each tenant's name listed in simple lettering. As she walked into the entryway, she smelled fresh lilac yet again in the dead of winter, even though Ms. Fontenot — the elderly lady who had the first-floor unit — said repeatedly that she did not keep fresh flowers in her apartment. Ada shared a glass of Chardonnay with her every week and had never seen a single flower, pot of potpourri or candle in her entire place. That left the doctor in the remaining unit. He was ruggedly handsome in a silver fox sort of way, and Ada was quite sure he was not a flowery sort of fellow. She checked her mail and headed up the stairs to her place.

Exhausted and weary to the bone, she couldn't wait to cuddle up with Mr. Jiggles.

When she put her hand on the knob of the door after unlocking it, she noticed it felt warm. *So weird.* This had happened a number of times before inexplicably, and she just couldn't explain it away or get used to it. A little shiver went up the back of her neck, and she shook it off as she walked into her apartment.

Mr. Jiggles greeted her with frenzied meows and demanded a pet and a snack. She threw her backpack on the dinette table and began rummaging through the fridge. In it was leftover tilapia Vera Cruz, half a bottle of dry white wine, and a few raspberry cheesecake turnovers from the bakery down the street. Even though a cup of tea had sounded delicious earlier, now that she was home and feeling exhausted, she decided on the dry white wine instead. She dumped the fish onto a clean plate and flaked off several bites for the cat into his glass bowl on the island. She tossed her plate into the microwave and hunted for a clean wine glass. All she could find was a green-leaded glass tumbler for cognac. *Oh well, who's to judge. Surely not Mr. Jiggles. Besides, he's been properly bribed with tilapia.* With the ding of the microwave she tossed a turnover on her plate with the fish, grabbed the tumbler of wine, and settled in front of the TV with a cozy chenille blanket.

Mr. Jiggles cuddled up in the crook between her thighs and breasts, cleaning his paws and purring with a vigor that could have woke the dead. She'd barely finished the fish and wine before she passed out in front of the TV.

Streaming beams of sunlight woke her the next morning. She appreciated the light from the French doors of her modest patio. Groggy, with a rumbling stomach, she brewed fresh coffee with her French press, languishing in the divine smell of a new imported Arabica she'd been dying to try out. She grabbed a carton of fresh cream and poured it into her cup. Mr. Jiggles appeared magically on the island next to her cup of coffee as if on cue after hearing the sound of the refrigerator door open. He started to reach one dainty white paw into her mug, but she scolded him, pouring some cream on a saucer for him instead. He eyed her contemptuously before he began lapping up his cream.

She was late with his breakfast and could see the cold disdain on his plump face. His gaze appraised her icily. Food seemed to consume his thoughts every waking moment, and his considerable girth attested to his obsession. She reached into the cabinet next to the fridge and got him a pouch of tuna. *Not cat food, human food. Mr. Jiggles has standards.* She dumped it onto his saucer, and he ate hungrily, as if he hadn't eaten in a week. She poured coffee into her cup, added a dash of Irish liquor, and took a hardy sip. The coffee flooded into her system, perking her up. The new Arabica was scrumptious.

After her dose of caffeine, Ada padded down the hall to her bedroom. The wooden floors felt cold on her feet, and it was clear winter's chill was coming. She rifled through her walk-in closet, finally emerging with a black cashmere twin set, lived-in skinny jeans, and black high-heeled boots. She grabbed a pair of simple black silk panties and a silk bra. After some rummaging around her jewelry box, she decided on black obsidian earrings. She padded into the bathroom and gingerly put her hand on the crystal knob. It was cold, like it should be. Relieved, she opened the door and flicked on the lights. The claw foot tub was original to the building, and it took up a massive amount of space in the bathroom. Black and white penny tiles decorated the floor and ran up to a simple tile bevel chair rail. She wondered if any of the painted women who worked in the brothel had bathed in her tub. *They must have.* She shuddered and turned on the shower. She stripped down and stepped into the spray, eager for the refreshing power of the water. After soaping every inch and covering her body with rose oil, she dressed. She combed her long hair and decided to let it air dry.

When she walked out into the living room, she saw Mr. Jiggles sunbathing himself by the patio doors after gorging himself on cream and tuna. She grabbed her backpack, pulled out her laptop and notepad, and tossed them on the coffee table. She poured some more coffee, then logged into the university website and began reading the syllabus for her new class in detail. Sipping her coffee, she pulled her twin set around her shoulders a little tighter. The air seemed to have dropped twenty degrees inexplicably. Steam swirled above her coffee cup in the chilled air, but Ada ignored the frigid room and continued reading the syllabus. A few pages in was the list of student pairings for the project. She took a deep breath and prayed she would not be assigned to the meathead—*or worse one of the dingy gold diggers.* When she discovered Chris was her partner, she let out a whoosh of air, relieved at the news. Her spirits rose as she anticipated spending more time with her newfound friend.

Mr. Jiggles turned and looked at her. He was oddly panting, even though she still felt a strange chill in her apartment. She got up and padded over to the thermostat. It was at seventy-eight degrees as usual. She shrugged off the weird temperature in her apartment and went back over to her laptop. After she found Chris' contact information, she saved it on her phone. Curious if he would be coming to the student study group at Boho Luna, she decided to drop him a text to confirm. An evening with the dingy girls and meathead was not appealing. An evening sitting in the back of the room with Chris, watching the blonde, brunette, and meat-head saga play out—priceless. She began reading the required chapters while her coffee was still hot, then researched the Vogue Theatre, the venue for their offsite lecture this Friday.

Time passed quickly, and before she knew it the grandfather clock in the corner rang, telling her it was already four in the afternoon. It was time to leave for Boho. A pumpkin spice coffee and a macadamia cookie sounded tempting. She popped into the bathroom and decided to apply a little makeup and some lipstick. She ran a brush through her hair and tried to tie it back in a ponytail. Half of her wild ringlets escaped despite her best efforts, so she gave up, letting her hair cascade down her back. It seemed like it grew every minute it was free from containment. Hurrying, she grabbed her backpack and jacket, then patted Mr. Jiggles on the way out. She locked her apartment and almost sprinted down the stairs.

The sun and fall air warmed her skin as she walked to her car. She took time to breathe in the fresh fall air and the scent of the leaves as she unlocked her car and tossed her things on the passenger seat. She was looking forward to Boho Luna, as it also had a very intriguing past. She'd spent some time that afternoon researching the numerous deaths and suicides that had occurred there. She'd read on a Vancouver ghost blog that occasionally the new owner gave tours of the upper floors where the incidents had occurred, but she'd also heard he wasn't always around, which might make it hard to investigate.

Ada had no trouble finding a parking space when she made it to Boho and only needed to walk one block to get to the cafe. As she walked in, she noticed the blonde from class. Her classmate was walking in front of her in a super short corduroy miniskirt paired with a flowered button-down blouse and chunky brown boots with crocheted knee-high socks popping out of the top. Ada noticed the blonde only had her purse. She had no backpack or notepad to take notes. She walked with her head down, texting someone with her monolith-sized cell. Ada inhaled and smelled her sweet perfume, booze and something else — the smell of sex. *Must be nice to be so loose and carefree! She spent her day drinking and getting laid, I spent my day studying — with my cat, no less.* She exhaled dramatically.

The entry to the café was just ahead — *thankfully*. Ada followed a bit behind the blonde so she wouldn't have to get too close to her and her aroma of fun. She scanned the room, eager to locate her new friend Chris. The wonderful smells of coffee and decadent desserts filled the air. Exposed brick and high ceilings with original hardwood floors and stainless steel gave the space a modernized vintage feel. As she walked across the wooden floors they creaked, and she could sense the history of the building. The air was heavy with an emotional weight that time could not wash away. Strange that her building was a former brothel, but its air was not tainted with heavy emotions from its past. This building, however, was very different. Despite the creepiness of the place, it was still packed with students. She saw Chris' tall figure in the back corner at a small table. As she made her way over to him, she realized he had already purchased a plate of snacks and two coffees.

"Wow great! My favorite macadamia nut cookies. You must have read my mind. Is this pumpkin spice?" She dipped her finger into the whipped topping.

"Absolutely. Who comes here and doesn't get a pumpkin spice latte? There are cranberry macaroons as well, my all-time favorite. My grandmother used to make almond cherry macaroons when I was a kid for our afternoon snack and for her bridge club. Boho's culinary creations really take me back to her kitchen.

"I really miss my grandparents. We were close. Nothing like Gram's peanut butter buttons." She sat down at the table and felt instantly grateful he chose this vantage point. She could see the entire room from this corner.

"Yeah, I was kind of a black sheep. The odd one in the family. Some other relatives were like me, so my grandparents knew I was odd before I even knew. They really took me under their wing." Chris sipped his coffee coolly, his round brown eyes peering over the rim of the cup. He appeared to be gauging her response to what he'd just admitted.

As shock washed over her, she sat her cup down with a thud and some sloshed out onto the saucer. "You're kidding! The same with me. The odd ones were my parents. My grandmother noticed right away I was one of the odd people that seem to periodically pop up in our family when I started having *the dreams.*"

The air began to feel heavy to Ada. Her mind drifted as she thought about the strangeness that filled both their pasts. Chris seemed to be doing the same. *Hopefully this class will be a break from reality, a little fun and no calculus.*

"So that's what you were trying to contain in your braid? You look sort of like a silky-headed curly troll doll, or maybe an 80's hooker. Go ahead, lick some more of that crème on the latte. That dude to your right is about to *crème* his jeans."

She noticed that his entire face lit up as he laughed.

He was teasing her like the brother she'd never had, and it felt nice. Her cheeks warmed in embarrassment as she slid out her notes. She took a sip of her latte, and the warm spiced sweetness instantly brightened her mood.

"Whoa, whoa, whoa lady. What's that?" He pointed at her notebook and eyed her with mock suspicion. "Do you think students come here to actually study?"

Ada's brows furrowed in mock annoyance before she smiled.

"I studied all day, actually. This place is bat-shit crazy haunted. There have been a bizarre number of unexplained deaths here and suicides." She paused for a moment.

"Remember those odd dreams I have sometimes? I've had some other unexplainable things happen as well. I hope this class can help me make sense of some of it." Ada lowered her head and became overly preoccupied with the filling in one of the macaroons, feeling vulnerable sharing her secrets.

"I don't want you to think I'm some kind of weird psychic fruitcake," she continued. "I bet you think you just won the partner jackpot. Meathead or one of the Labradors are probably looking really good about now." She glanced at Chris, nervously waiting for his reply.

"No way. I am very open minded about the paranormal. Like I said before, I've had my share of the unexplained happen. Well, truthfully probably much more than most people. I also took the class with the hope that I could shed some light on some of those incidents."

Relief flooded across Ada's face and she smiled back at her new partner. "I heard the owner takes students on tours of the building, but I didn't see him around today. I cyber-stalked him this morning, and he looks like an older version of meathead."

Chris eyed the stairs warily before giving her a conspiratorial smile. "Well, I noticed a sign when I came in that the bathroom is upstairs. I searched the internet a little, too, this morning, and most of the stories I read said many of the paranormal occurrences are upstairs. Although I hardly made a whole notebook of notes — like someone else."

He gestured slightly derisively at her notebook as he peered out over his coffee cup. He choked out a coffee-soaked laugh despite his obvious efforts to appear serious. When he calmed down, he twisted around and looked behind him.

"See that sign around the back pointing up? Looks like we will have to take an unguided tour when we get lost looking for the bathroom, to, you know, pee after we drink all this coffee. It's not because that kid hung himself in there last semester or anything like that." Chris smiled at her and winked, his perfect teeth glinting with a slight shark-like edge. He gestured subtly across the room. "In the mean-time we can enjoy our coffees and watch the meathead drama play out."

Ada looked over Chris's burly shoulder and, sure enough, there sat blondie and brunette together with meathead the next table over. Meathead appeared disinterested in the discussion the only other guy at the table was attempting to have with him. The second guy just happened to be a well-known super nerd on campus with pop bottle glasses and cystic acne. Ada had many classes with said nerd, and he was indeed the consummate student. The professor had clearly paired jock with super-nerd to keep the dean happy and meathead playing football.

Ada turned her attention to the blonde and brunette. She noticed they were predictably engrossed with one of their enormously-sized smartphones. *Probably trolling the skanks of Instagram to gauge the competition.* The brunette was wearing the usual too-tight clothing and shoes that matched her outfit. It was very apparent that they were not studying. The brunette started laughing and pointing at something on her phone, and the blonde followed suit. Ada guzzled some coffee, as if the caffeine could prevent her from losing IQ points by being in the room with meathead and his mustard-yellow and chocolate-brown Labradors. She munched her macaroon and scanned the now crowded bar with a cursory glance. A sneaky mission upstairs started to appeal to her.

"Ready to find the restrooms? I truly have to tinkle." She smiled mischievously at Chris.

Chapter Three: The Epiphany

Ada slinked up the stairs first, alone, with Chris following shortly after her. As she waited for him at landing and bend in the stairs, she couldn't help but take in the shoddy and depressing state of the stairwell. The stairs were the original wood, stained a dark walnut tone. They were probably lovely at some point but just looked worn now. Chris finally caught up with her, the stairs creaking and complaining under Chris' significant frame.

As she made it to the top, she came to a long hallway with high ceilings and several antique doors that looked original to the building, with glass transoms above them. The air seemed to be twenty degrees cooler on this floor. She shivered and pulled her sweater closer to her body and folded her arms across her chest. The sign for the men's room and ladies' room were hanging from the ceiling with lettering in an antique cast iron. She placed her hand on the brass doorknob and jerked her hand away as soon as her skin felt the frigidly cold metal. It almost burned her. She pulled her sweater down over her hand and tried the handle again. The door groaned and opened to a bathroom that looked the same as it must have in the twenties. There were art deco tiles and a lovely Carrara marble sink, monogrammed BL towels. *Elaborate, for a coffee shop.* The unmistakable odor of an old home wafted through the open door. She held her breath and walked in, with every nerve in her body tingling. And then . . . absolutely nothing happened. She twirled around and took one final look around. It was simply an old bathroom in an old home.

She walked back out into the hallway and met Chris, who was waiting outside the men's room door, leaning his back against the wall. Ada realized how narrow the hallway was and how tall the ceilings were. His hulking frame nearly took up the full width of the hall. *I wonder if all of him is that big.* Blushing she put the thought out of her mind. She smiled at him mischievously, praying silently that he could not read her mind.

"Anything interesting in the men's room? I think that's where that kid hung himself. Unless there's another bathroom up here." Clutching her sweater tighter around her shoulders, she shivered yet again. "I found nothing in the ladies room. Unless you count frigid air and musty old home smell as something worth noting."

"Absolutely nothing remarkable about the men's room. Some old tile work and original fixtures. I poked around, and I couldn't figure out where someone might have hung themselves. Maybe it's not the right room. Let's keep going."

They looked down the hall at several nondescript doors. Sunlight streamed through the transom of the door on the far end. It seemed to beckon them closer, as if the door itself had life. She pointed at the furthest door.

"How about that one, Chris? It must be an important room, because it has a hinged transom, and the others don't have a hinge. The transom windows above interior doors were used back in the day to circulate hot air out of the house. So all rooms that weren't closets typically had them in more sophisticated homes. They also positioned exterior windows to create a cross breeze. It was an early form of air conditioning that only the elite could afford.

"Plus I read two deaths occurred in the same bedroom, nearly a hundred years apart. There were more deaths on the third floor as well."

She smiled at him and made her best miss-know-it-all face.

"Bet you appreciate my research now, since we are snooping."

Chris shook his head and looked down at his shoes, smiling smugly.

They walked single file down the hallway with Chris in the lead. He put his hand on the knob and gave it a twist. They both held their breath, terrified they would walk in on something and the owner would throw them out, or worse, call the police.

He opened the door, revealing a dusty storage room with shelving full of supplies for the shop. There was an old lumpy sofa and a television on a dilapidated Formica TV stand. A coffee table that looked like it came straight out of a thrift shop was centered in front of the sofa on an old rainbow sisal rug. The table had a big chunk missing out of one corner and teetered precariously to the left on an uneven leg. There was a huge rip in the black velvet back of the sofa and cigarette burn holes on it as well. That was when she realized this must be some of the original furniture from the house's frat days. Aware that objects sometimes retained residue from traumatic events, she wondered if the furniture might have something to do with the alleged haunting activity.

Before she could go near the sofa, though, familiar giggles resounded down the hallway, along with meathead's voice and the sound of clumping boots. Chris looked at her with equal panic written on his face, and they frantically searched for a different way out of the room. There were a set of louvred doors on the other side of the room, but no other exit. They tip toed to the closet, and she tried the doors. No luck, they wouldn't budge. Chris tried the doors again. He was becoming rapidly more alarmed as the giggles and thuds from the hallway became louder. They didn't budge. Finally he pushed his shoulder into the doors in the opposite direction. They burst open, revealing an empty closet just large enough for them to hide inside. They slipped inside and shut the doors. She exhaled a huge sigh of relief. Images of the police arresting them for trespassing played through her mind as she tried to stay quiet.

The louvred slats didn't completely block their view of the main room. Meathead stumbled into the room first, followed by blondie and the brunette. Ada looked at Chris and slapped her hand over her mouth, feeling like they were voyeuristic co-conspirators. She stifled a giggle with her hand as it threatened to bubble to the surface.

The trio was sloppy drunk with the unmistakable stench of cheap liquor announcing their arrival almost before they entered the room. The brunette smiled at the lumbering jock as she flipped her ponytail over her shoulder and rubbed her perky breasts against his arm. The blonde poured some of the contents of her water bottle into a mug meathead was holding.

"Hey girls, how about I show you where one of the suicides happened? You know it happened in this v-very room." Meathead stumbled and slurred his words, nearly spilling the contents of his mug. It sloshed over the rim onto the blonde's surprisingly full breasts. She wiped it away and licked it off her beautifully manicured fingers erotically.

The girls glanced at each other, flashing mischievous smiles at each other. They seemed to have ideas other than classwork in mind.

"There are other, more fun things we could do to occupy ourselves, Kevin," the brunette said as she shut the door behind them and twisted the old brass lock. The sound of the tumblers echoed across the room as clicking loudly into place.

Kevin turned and looked at her, his eyes wide with mock surprise. "Is this a closed-door meeting, Dana? To discuss the paranormal activity of the second floor for class? Do you think the ghost likes watching anal sex? Or maybe just a good old-fashioned titty fuck?"

Dana smiled deviously, twirling her dark hair.

"How about you show us what you think the ghost likes best, Dana. Maybe a little girl on girl? I got a little sneak preview of Kari's best assets earlier. How would you like to evaluate them? In the name of science, of course, to see what the ghost prefers. Big titty blondes or feisty brunettes? A good ass fuck or a little titty fuck? What do you say ladies?"

Kevin shifted from one foot to the other as the bulge in his pants became visible even from Ada's vantage point in the closet. *No way. They wouldn't. This is not happening!*

Dana walked over to the sofa near the coffee table where the other two were standing. Kari chugged the liquid in her water bottle and handed it to Dana, who took a huge swig as well, her face puckering in response to the obviously cheap booze.

Lumbering a bit closer to the women Kevin, struggled to drunkenly slur out a few more words. "Now ladies, let's take a look at Kari's new assets."

He unbuttoned Kari's blouse, exposing a demure white bra that was attempting to contain two augmented breasts which were a tad too large for her small frame. Kevin ran his hands over her firm, round breasts. Only a delicate bow and clasp at the front contained her generous breasts. He unhooked it slowly, exposing her erect pale pink nipples. He squeezed them lightly and stepped aside. Kevin unbuckled his jeans and pulled them down.

Ada watched as a warm trickle of his seed escaped his engorged shaft.

"Do you think they are too big, from one girl to another?" Kari asked, running her hands over her nipples, cupping her breasts and arching her back. "Do you think they feel too firm?"

Kari reached out, grabbed Dana's hand, and pulled it up to

her breast. Dana cupped them together and ran her hands over Kari's nipples, inciting a subtle sigh from her friend. Kevin walked over to the shelves full of supplies and grabbed a bottle of what looked like olive oil. He walked back to the couch, poured olive oil on his hand and began stroking his cock.

Ada's mouth dropped open, and she turned to face Chris. He looked equally shocked. Kevin was very well endowed in the package region, and Ada began to realize there was more than one reason the ladies flocked to him.

Dana pressed her body up against Kari's and kissed her once chastely on the lips, then began to kiss her with carnal desire, on par with a sexually hungry male. As Dana's hungry, rough kiss escalated, she squeezed Kari's breasts and nipples, making her moan in ecstasy. She devoured her neck, leaving red traces of her lipstick down to her chest. Dana pushed one breast up and into her mouth and began to suckle a nipple. Kari wrapped one long leg around Dana and grabbed both of her hips rubbing her hips against her.

"Dana, why don't you test out how fresh Kari is down there, taste her, and let's see if our ghost likes oral. Fuck her with your tongue, and with those long pretty fingers of yours." Kevin's voice was thick with arousal. He stroked his engorged cock as he watched the two co-eds.

From their vantage point in the closet, Ada and Chris could see everything through the slats and could not stop watching. As Dana pushed up Kari's skirt higher to meet Kevin's requests, Ada's jaw dropped. She turned and looked at Chris, who had covered his mouth to stifle a giggle that clearly threatened to burst out at any moment. As much as she thought she shouldn't watch what was about to happen with meathead and the Labradors, it was like not watching a train wreck unfold. She couldn't stop herself. She turned her head back to the unfolding threesome with her mouth still open in shock.

Dana pushed the skirt up Kari's surprisingly meaty hip, exposing her bare, hairless coral pink box. No panties. She left one hand on Kari's breast and slid one hand down to her dripping wet clitoris. She carefully caressed the hood of her clitoris with two fingers and jammed her knee between Kari's legs, spreading them wide.

"You've been a bad girl today Kari, haven't you? I can smell sex on you. Just for that, we are going to fuck you hard, until you scream. Both of us. Kevin and me. Maybe at the same time, you dirty little bitch."

She squeezed her breast harder, and Kari squealed. Dana's bag was lying on the couch, and she rifled through it. She pulled out a shockingly large dildo and a small whip.

"Kevin, take the whip."

Kari's eyes grew round. Dana got on her knees, cupped both of Kari's bare ass cheeks, and took in her scent. She ran her tongue over her clitoris. Dana suckled softly on her clitoris then harder, as she began to moan. She left one delicate kiss on the lips of her friend's box and looked up into Kari's eyes. Then, Dana kissed Kari's box deeper, sliding her tongue into its opening. Kari grabbed the back of her head and pushed Dana's face further into her vagina. Kari thrust her tongue deep into her box at that moment, and the warm wet thrusting made Kari's orgasm spray from her box and drip down Dana's chin. Kari's erotic squeals of ecstasy pulsed with Dana's tongue as she became intoxicated with the throws of her orgasm.

Kevin began swatting Kari's meaty hip with the whip until her hip was raw and red. He grabbed the back of Dana's head and pushed it harder into Kari's box. He got down on his knees behind Dana and pressed his lips up against her ear.

"Fuck her harder. I want to hear her scream."

He switched his whip to his other hand and began

whipping Dana's ass. He grabbed the back of her yoga pants and pulled them down, exposing her plain black thong. He grabbed the back of her hips and pressed his cock against her back. He slid his free hand under the back of her thong until he reached to her anus, then slid one oiled finger into it. Dana jumped as it penetrated her. He pulled it back out and licked it. Kevin stood up and pulled Dana's shirt over her head, exposing her naked and pendulous breasts. She rarely wore a bra, and today was no exception.

He reached over and pulled Kari's skirt down over her boots and pushed her onto the couch. He pulled the skirt the rest of the way off, and now she lay naked on the couch except for her unbuttoned blouse and the boots. She spread her legs apart in anticipation, slipping one finger inside her box, and one hand rubbed a breast hungrily. Dana had pulled her pants the rest of the way off and she was naked except for her thong.

She got down on her knees and pulled Kevin's pants and shoes completely off, so all that remained was his sweatshirt. She pulled it over his head and off as well, then stopped for a second to catch her breath.

Ada's breath caught loudly in the closet as well, so loudly she was afraid they might've heard her. Kevin was gorgeous. He was thickly muscled with a thin waist, taught ass, and a large cock. It almost looked painfully large. He had the body of a Greek God.

Ada could almost feel Chris' scrutiny as she ogled Kevin, his head cocked sideways as he looked at her. She turned to him, and he shook his head, stifling a giggle. Ada made the shush motion with one finger held up to her lips. She looked back through the slats, eager to see the rest of the show.

Dana placed her knees on the couch in between Kari's open legs. She slid two fingers inside Kari and began to pump her. Kari's rhythmic moans were interrupted by the sound of

Kevin striking Dana's naked ass with the whip.

"Harder, fuck her harder. I want to hear this dirty bitch scream."

He cracked the whip down on Dana's ass cheek so hard it made her jump. She turned around to look at him, and he studied the large phallus for a moment before taking it from her. He poured olive oil over the dildo and slid his hand up and down over it, completely covering it. "Dirty bitch, do you think you can take all of this?"

He brandished the dildo once more and handed it to Dana. Dana slid it into Kari, and she screamed in total shock. As Dana thrust it into her, Kari looked like she was going to have have another orgasm. As Kari's screams escalated, Kevin mounted Dana from behind and slipped into her vagina. Dana winced for a second as her body accommodated his girth, then she too began to moan. Kari let out a screech before gushing all over the couch. Soon after Dana climaxed, too. She collapsed at the opposite end of the couch after Kevin pulled out of her.

Then Kevin went over to Kari and began to fondle her breasts. She sat up against the back of the armrest and arched her back. He straddled her and rubbed his erect cock against her breasts and nipples. He poured olive oil on her breasts, smashing them together while pushing his cock between them. He then proceeded to titty fuck her with vigor. Ada watched from her vantage point in the closet as his tight ass and muscled back pumped against Kari's breasts. Just as his moans began to gain momentum, he pulled his cock out from between her breasts and grabbed her head. He slid his cock into her mouth and exploded seconds later into her mouth. He sat back on the sofa afterwards, his head lolled back in total exhaustion.

Ada was now staring slack jawed through the louvres at the spectacle that had just gone down. Needless to say, this was not what she, nor Chris probably, expected to encounter on the second floor. Maybe some weird drafts, creaky floors or slammed doors. Definitely not a crazy juicy orgy complete with whips featuring meathead. She looked over at Chris and saw her expression reflected all over his face. Now it was Ada's turn to place a hand over her mouth to stifle a giggle as she looked at Chris, whose eyebrows had somehow almost reached his hairline in shock. *How are we going to get out of this closet? Are these people done? Please say they aren't up for another round.*

Her thoughts were racing and her heart was pounding. She looked back through the louvres in time to see meathead dressing. He hopped on one foot pulling on his pants and plopped down on the coffee table to slip on his shoes. Dana began dressing and gathering her things, too. She reached out and shook Kari's shoulder to rouse her.

"I could use some pizza and a beer." Kari exhaled as she sat up, blowing her hair out of her face. *Probably in exhaustion.*

Meathead looked at her incredulously, as if he couldn't fathom why this woman thought she deserved a beer from him, *the prince*. It was as if she hadn't just fulfilled every man's ultimate threesome fantasy. He grabbed Kari's face and squeezed her cheeks in his beefy hands. He lowered his face to hers. Cupping his cock inside his pants with his free hand to better convey his feelings on the matter, he carefully enunciated his words as if speaking to a child.

"Baby, you know what? You can have my cock in the morning after practice, when I'm all hot and sweaty. I'll even cum in your mouth. How's that sound for a snacky poo?"

He grabbed her head and rubbed her face against the rough material of his pants encasing his cock, already firming up again at the prospect of Kari's mindless lips wrapping around him. Dana rolled her eyes, her annoyance with meathead palpable. She cleared her throat and cocked her head to the side, staring into meathead's blank eyes.

"Kari, let's go get a drink. The first one is on me. The second one will be on the random hot guy at the bar who wants to buy you one. Or both of us one." With that statement, Kari winked at Dana and grabbed her purse. The girls slinked out the door and down the hall, their footsteps loudly echoing. A snarky giggle wafted its way back to Ada and Chris before they finally heard the sound of the bulky football player walking out of the room and down the hall. Chris and Ada waited tensely for a few minutes to make sure they were truly alone before bursting out of the closet.

Ada's sensibilities were a little shaken. *I've never even seen a porno. Or had sex!* It wasn't because of lack of opportunity or interested men. She'd just never felt that way about anyone, man or woman thus far in her life. She knew it was odd, but there was nothing to be done about it.

She inhaled deeply and wrinkled her nose. The room smelled. The scent of carnal sex hung in the air. Her face was flushed with embarrassment at what they'd just witnessed, albeit unintentionally. She raised her hands to either side of her face, feeling the heat of a flush rise to her skin.

"Did that just happen?" Her voice rose an octave or two towards the end of the words.

"I feel dirty. Like *I* need a shower. That was steamier than any porno I've ever watched, and I'm embarrassed to say I've seen my fair share." Chris laughed nervously, still a little afraid they would get caught.

"Let's go before they come back for another round. I could really use a drink to process all of that. I mean geeez, Chris, how will we look them in the eye during class now?"

She stammered on in astonishment that bordered on stunned hysteria. "I just saw ALL of meathead, and all the lady parts of the two Labradors, chocolate and yellow." She gestured dramatically at her groin area, eyes wide. "I think I could have done without some of that visual, I must say."

It was Chris' turn to weigh in on the carnage. He seemed equally astonished. "Did you see the size of meathead's, um, *dick*? Who would have guessed that was all buttoned up in his pants? And the whip! People really do that! And like it?"

Ada nodded, agreeing with Chris' sentiments. She took another sniff of the air in the room and saw the tipped over bottle of olive oil now drenching the wood floor in front of the couch. *This must be how mystery stains happen on old hardwood.* She wrinkled her nose and looked around the room before clearing her throat to speak again.

"I wonder what the spirits thought of what happened. I'd say it's a given that they all must have been the somber sullen sort . . . since many of the deaths were ruled suicides or deemed accidents."

She reached out and touched the intricate detailing in the woodwork around the massive windows. The battered and peeling paint was oddly cold to the touch, despite the warm afternoon sun streaming in through the window. A high-pitched crackling sound pierced the lazy afternoon air, growing louder and more intense. Time slowed to a crawl, and Ada felt the hair stand up on the back of her neck. She looked up at the top of the window to see a transom develop spider-web like cracks, just before the pane underneath it began to break as well.

Chris grabbed Ada around her tiny waist and pulled her back. yanking her off her feet just as the entire transom burst and glass shards rained down exactly where she'd been standing. He fell back and she toppled over him, landing in his lap.

Just then the rest of the panes below the transom also burst spraying shards of glass into the room. A high-pitched ping cut through the sound of the spraying shards and the window next to that one also began to shatter. She felt Chris's strong hands grab her as he pulled them both up to their feet.

Lunging towards the door, he pushed her in front of him.

"Run!"

They booked it down the hallway and down the stairs, taking them two at a time. They grabbed their stuff from their table and exited unceremoniously as quickly as possible before someone noticed what had happened upstairs or worse yet, blamed it on them.

Chapter Four: Provocation

The loud drone from the boisterous students in the coffee shop must have drowned out the chaos upstairs — all of it, the sex, the windows, the running feet. Everything happening downstairs looked status quo as they hurried outside. As if not a single sound had been heard. The fresh air struck Ada's face, and she took a deep breath as they hurried down the street towards her car. She looked at her newfound friend's face with reverence. She could have been killed or maimed by that glass.

He had an angry scowl and a sternness spreading across his handsomely chiseled face.

"I'm parked just down here. Would you like to get a drink at O'Malley's? They have a legendary Irish car bomb. I think I could use about a dozen of them right now."

When they made it to her sedan, Ada nearly dropped her keys because her hands were shaking so badly.

"Why don't I drive?" Chris grabbed picked up the keys and ushered her into the passenger's seat, tossing her bag in the back seat.

He flashed his perfectly white smile at her, all signs of his earlier scowl and sternness dissipated. He enjoyed having someone to look after. Chris realized that he liked helping her and being her savior as he slid his hulking body into the driver's seat. He turned to Ada and looked deeply into her eyes. She stared back with her round, brown eyes which still appeared a little too wide and slightly bewildered.

"I think it's safe to say that the Boho Luna is actually haunted. On a side note, it's also safe to say the ghost, or ghosts, whoever he, she, or *it* is, doesn't like group sex. But why did it go after you instead of them? Was it watching and enjoying the show? Or was it calling us out for staying in the closet for the show?"

He flicked a little piece of glass out of her riotous hair and saw a small shard in her neck. "Hold still. There's a little one in your neck."

"What? In my neck?"

Chris could see panic rising in her delicate face. The panic began to set in, but before she could have a full-blown minute, the fleck of glass was gone and he was dotting the blood with a handkerchief from his pocket.

"See, no big deal. Just a little prick."

With that she finally started to giggle. She laughed so hard he saw tears begin to form in the corners of her eyes. Chris joined in, letting out all the leftover anxious energy pent up inside him. He was really glad he'd met her. She finally stopped laughing and turned to look at him. She had a slightly bewildered look on her face. "Wow, what a huge . . . dick. Did you see the size of meathead's salami? He's also a bigger asshole than I'd ever expected."

She shook her head side to side. Her eyebrows were raised and her round brown eyes met his gaze.

He chuckled. It was good to see her making light of the situation.

"You like my bad jokes?" she asked as a half-smile flashed across her face. He noticed that her eyes smiled too.

"I'll give it to you, meathead has a large dick. But as a dude, I can't say that is all that remarkable. I personally was kind of shocked to see Kari's, umm, assets are a lot more artificial than I thought they would be. But I really hadn't studied them much, mostly because she is such a simpleton, and that is really unattractive. Don't get me wrong, most men would be happy with her body. It's beautiful. But her mind is missing quite a lot."

He noticed Ada's face grew somber as she mulled something over in her mind. Sensing she had something to say, he waited a moment to put the car in gear. She finally chimed in with her thoughts.

"Kevin's mind is shockingly dark. He had zero interest in either of those girls on a personal level. He was all about getting his dirty fantasy needs met. I really just assumed he was a vacuous jock, but he's actually an asshole too."

"Yeah, that surprised me, too. I thought the same, that he was just a dumb jock and a rich kid with more money than sense."

With that he pulled the car away from the curb and they were on their way to the pub. He was eager to put distance between them and the Boho Luna.

There was a happy energy inside the car. Something was different, and Ada couldn't quite put her thumb on it. But despite almost being maimed by glass shards, she was still happy she'd met Chris. They seemed to be on the same wavelength. A real friend she could confide in was something she was missing in life. She wasn't sure of what to make of the dirty group sex and whip, but she wasn't totally sorry she'd seen it, either.

They also had some answers on whether ghosts existed or not—however, she'd already known they were real. She'd signed up for the class to see if anyone else knew as much as she did, and to meet people with experience with the great beyond. She did not think for a second that the shattering glass was any sort of coincidence.

So much was happening, and her mind was spinning. She was also still quite curious about Mathias. If he was teaching this course, he must have some insight or personal interest in the subject matter. *So what is his motivation behind teaching such a controversial course? Most professors would be afraid to be considered crazy coots if they taught it. So what's his deal?*

They pulled up to the pub just as the sun was setting and a frigid edge to the air was setting in. She couldn't help but think that winter was really here. As they made it through the doors, she realized that lots of other students were inside combating winter's first chill with a drink. She felt Chris' hand on the small of her back, ushering her towards the bar.

After they spent a few minutes standing at the bar with their drinks and making small talk, a booth finally opened-up at the back. They made their way through the crowd and huddled together. It was deep, and the cushions were cracked and lumpy at best. After a few drinks, neither of them noticed the uncomfortable seats. The conversation evolved from small talk to more serious discussions about the course and hauntings in general.

Ada opened her heart a little to Chris. After all, he had just saved her life. She explained that her parents passed and her grandmother raised her on their family farm outside Vancouver. She began to explain how some odd things had happened to her over the years.

"Like what?" Chris asked, fully engrossed in their conversation.

"For example, I've had dreams about things that happen before they happen. Sometimes I have odd feelings that are sort of like warnings, and of course there are the real life slow mos. Time is fluid for me. Sometimes it just seems to stop or slow down. I have some control over when it happens, but for a long time I didn't. My mind is at a normal pace, or a hyper pace, but everything else slows or stops. People, animals, clocks, everything.

"Also things like the window incident from today aren't all that unusual. Back home I completely stopped going to one of my friend's houses as well as the church because there was some sort of residual something going on or maybe an active something. I don't know which."

She smiled at him, realizing she'd been rambling and looked down into the bottomless pool of her drink. Outing her quirky life was cathartic but embarrassing as well. "You are probably writing me off right this second as a bat-shit crazy person, and I wouldn't blame you. Have you ever had any personal experiences with anything paranormal? You know, ghosts and the unexplainable?

She felt her cheeks flush crimson as she looked up into Chris' fawn-colored eyes, fully expecting disgust or confusion after her bare-it-all admissions.

Instead, he was smiling at her and nodding his head emphatically. He took a huge swig of liquid courage before he began. "Au contraire, Miss Ada. Not only have I *personally* experienced all the things you've mentioned, I can one up you. Time slows down for me, too, with a few exceptions to what happens to you. I have quite a bit of control over when time slows or stops, and my *events* include extra strength. When I was eight, I pushed a car that had rolled over my dad's leg when he was under it tinkering. It crushed his femur, and he could have bled out from the femoral artery, if I hadn't thought on my feet.

"I remember it like it was yesterday. After I pushed the car off, I pulled him out from under the car, took his belt off and wrapped it around his thigh as a makeshift tourniquet. Then I called 911. All of this took twenty seconds, according to my dad. I weighed about sixty pounds back then. My dad was an easy two-hundred-and-sixty pounds. When the EMT's got there a cop showed up as well, and no one accepted or believed our story."

He looked down into his drink, his features contemplative as he recalled those difficult days.

Ada stared at him rapt with attention.

"As time passed, I realized that not only was no one like me, I was changing. My extra talents were changing and evolving. After the car incident. my grandmother sat me down and told me about her sister, Ester, who had long passed, but also had unusual talents like mine."

Ada sipped her coffee. She was stunned to hear his story. He was like her. Different, but the same.

"Grandma Ester was rumored to have pulled a pony — yes a pony — out of a pond where it was stuck in the muck at their farm. It was her favorite pony, and the family lore holds that this same pony never went near another body of water. Not that ponies aren't smart, but it seemed like someone told the pony water was a bad idea. Interestingly enough, I also found out later I could calm both people and animals. First it was by touch, then eventually, physical contact was no longer required.

"My grandmother never elaborated on whether or not she or her sister had met anyone else like Ester. There were a number of people who decided we were total crackpots in the small town where we lived. Our entire extended family was ostracized because of it. Eventually, everyone in our family stopped discussing Ester's *events*, even Ester herself. She marginalized herself and her abilities.

He studied his drink and picked at the crumbs on the plate in front of him. His facial expression was serious as he reflected upon the memories.

Ada waited impatiently as he gathered his thoughts. She was fully engrossed in his story and she felt as if every nerve ending was on edge.

"I took this class for much of the same reason you took it, Ada. I wanted to see if there was an explanation for Ester and me. The odd eye color, can that be explained? I never dreamed I was going to meet someone like me. So, to answer your question, no, I don't think you are bat-shit crazy. Maybe a bit anxious, but not full on bat-shit crazy."

Tears rolled down Ada's cheeks. Her heart was swelling with emotion. She never expected that there were others. She decided, after brief contemplation, to share a story with him about her early experiences.

"I remember mine started with a bizarre ability to empathize with other people. Not a normal empathy, but like a glimpse into their soul. Just a snapshot of the happiest parts of their lives and the worst parts as well. I was five, and I would read the cashier's mind at the grocery store.

"The prophetic dreams came later. Sometimes they were nightmares, or so I thought. After the dreams, the real-time slow-mos started happening randomly. This was the most disconcerting and troubling of all *talents*.

She glanced at Chris from the corner of her eye. He was watching her with the same level of intensity she'd had for his stories. She exhaled and continued.

"I had no control over it initially. It has been and remains a huge source of anxiety for me. Now, I can control it sometimes, but every inch of power I gained over my talents took me a long time. As soon as I make progress it seems like something new comes up."

Chris placed his hand over her shoulder. It was massive and enveloped her delicate frame in comforting warmth. His touch reminded her that she wasn't in this alone anymore.

"Do you ever wonder what is going to happen next? I know your talents have evolved like mine, but sometimes it seems they pop out of nowhere overnight. I just wish I had some control. I still find it unhinging at its worst and unsettling at best. I guess it would be nice to find a useful balance."

She lowered her head and leaned in after looking around

to see if anyone was eavesdropping. Even though the coast was clear, she began to whisper.

"Do you ever wonder what could we do with our talents? If we could harness them, we could — I don't know — help people. Maybe? My dreams . . . I have these weird dreams that represent a possible version of the future. Sometimes they are correct, sometimes not, but always a representation of a possible reality. A while back I discovered I could focus on a topic that I was concerned about during bedtime, and I would be given answers during my dreams at night. The answers were hard to interpret sometimes, and many were more like nightmares than sweet dreams."

Chris took another swig of his drink and flagged down the waitress for another round. He smiled, and she noticed a slightly mischievous glint in his eye.

"We could start a 1-800 psychic line."

"Not funny, Chris. Too early."

They both laughed and it felt so good. Her heart felt lighter since she'd met him. *What would life be like right now without him? Where would I be right now? Home with my cat, again? Thinking I'm a total whack job?*

"Ooh! I have a legit idea. Tonight, let's try and think about the Boho Luna and see what dreams come to us. We could research the suicides at the café and see if that information gives us a focusing point for the dreams as well. I'm not sure I'm ready to go back to that café, but we could see how things go. Play it by ear."

Ada nodded, consenting to Chris' plan. They decided to call it a night, before they both had too much to drink, to test out their new theories. Ada drove Chris to his place and dropped him off.

Chapter Five: Advances

By the time she pulled up to her apartment, she was still keyed up from the events earlier in the day and could think of nothing but a nice hot cup of jasmine tea. The moment Ada stepped out of her car, she noticed the air smelled musty. It had an almost palpable dampness. A low rumble in the distance along with a not-so-subtle crack of lightening cut across the sky. Ada looked up and down the street as she walked toward the door to her apartment building. It seemed darker out than usual. When she entered the foyer, she noticed the hall light wasn't on, and the air was markedly chillier inside than when she'd left. She pulled her sweater across her chest tighter and went to check on her mailbox.

The moment her key entered the antique box, time slowed, and she heard every squeak and scrape of the lock as the tumblers clicked into place. *Oh for Pete's sake, not again. I just want a cup of tea and to get into some pajamas.* Her thoughts began to instinctively speed up with thoughts of doom and gloom. *This is never good.*

She heard the old doorknob to Ms. Fontenot's door turning. Ada heard the sound of her own hair rustling against her clothing, echoing in her own ears as her head whipped around. The old lady's apartment appeared extremely dark, and she was carrying not one, but two lit candles in antique copper holders. The copper was adorned with a round globe of a dark stone that appeared similar to onyx but had flecks of gold tones.

"There you are, dear. I've been up waiting for you to come

45

in. Powers been out since early this evening. I left some wood by your door for the fireplaces in your apartment so you'd stay cozy. Looks like a doozey of a storm rolling in, not sure when the power will come back on."

Time had returned to normal when Ms. Fontenot began to speak, leaving Ada puzzled. Ms. Fontenot walked to her slowly, her steps almost cat-like — which had always surprised her considering, Ms. Fontenot's advanced age. She handed Ada the candle and smiled.

"The power, it hasn't gone out since you moved in until today, has it?" Delia cocked her head to the side and squinted as she tried to remember.

"Nope, not once. It's sweet of you to bring me a candle, Ms. Fontenot." She made an effort to smile at her warmly even though she was thoroughly creeped out. The time slows were always a little unnerving, and today was no exception.

"Oh, your cat has been yowling up a storm up there since the power went out. I thought cats were supposed to like nighttime? Well then, I've got to get to bed for some beauty sleep. Takes work to keep this up."

With that she fluffed her over-sprayed hair and giggled. She retreated back to her apartment with the same slow but cat-like, almost gliding gate she always exhibited.

She is so damned weird. Shaking her head, Ada walked up to her apartment and couldn't help but think about how creepy this old building was in the dark. She loved it with all its character, but right now it was *not* very appealing. It looked identical to every horror movie she'd ever seen in the dark. She tried to shake off her fear, but a knot still remained in her throat.

The sound of her cat's insistent meows was a welcome distraction as they broke the eerie silence, his voice growing louder with every step as she drew closer to the door to her apartment. She made it up to her door, and the cat stuffed his entire fat paw under the door as soon as she started to unlock it. She found herself laughing as he purred and rubbed against her legs as if he was famished and hadn't eaten in a week. She walked in and put the candle on the counter along with her bag before heading back to the hallway to retrieve the bundle of wood from Ms. Fontenot. It was indeed cold in the apartment. The air was so frigid she could see her breath.

She took half the wood to the living room fireplace, and the other half she put beside the fireplace in the master bedroom. The wood was dry and caught fire very quickly. The flames brightened the apartment up, but it felt creepy. She undressed and put on snuggly pastel-plaid pajamas.

Eager for a pot of tea, she wandered into the kitchen and put the kettle on the stove. Thankfully, it was a gas stove. She fed the cat some dry food, much to his disdain. Not about to go hungry despite the substandard fare, he gobbled it down with the same zeal he seemed to show all food. Ada plopped down on the sofa and realized how weary she was after such a long day. Still, she felt alert and was unable to fully unwind. She hoped the tea would help soothe her rattled nerves.

She turned her attention to the strange candle holder from Ms. Fontenot. There was no wifi, so she began researching on her phone. She discovered it resembled polished hematite, treasured for years by local tribal populations. She turned it this way and that, the flames catching in glimmers across the smooth surface. She ran her hands across the smooth stone and found it warm, warmer than the room in fact. *Well, isn't that strange.* Just then the tea kettle whistled, and she padded into the kitchen. The cat was still chowing down on his supper, making loud crunching noises accompanied by gobbling sounds.

She reached into the cabinet, pulled out an old tin canister, and popped the lid off. She took a whiff of the tea leaves and was instantly comforted by the swirling vanillas and tranquilizing aroma of fresh loose-leaf tea. After rummaging around in a drawer, she located a stainless-steel tea-ball infuser. She loaded up the ball and dropped it into an enormous ceramic coffee mug. She poured the steaming water from the kettle into her cup. Hot steam spread the delicious aroma of vanilla tea through her apartment, and she decided some candied vanilla-roasted almonds would be lovely with the tea. She found some in the cabinet and poured them on the saucer next to her coffee mug.

She went back to the living room to find Mr. Jiggles settled in his usual spot on the sofa cuddled up on the cream-colored chenille blanket. He was purring and licking his paws, having forgotten his previous annoyance over the dry food. She grabbed the free end of the blanket and curled up underneath it. A deep satisfied sigh disrupted Mr. Jiggles' purring as he popped his head up to look at her. Within seconds he was back to a happily purring and kneading the blanket with his fat little paws.

The storm began to rage outside but she was too tired to notice. She sipped her tea and munched on the roasted almonds. She started to mull over the events at the Boho Luna. She thought back to the feelings she had when the windows began to crack. It had started when she touched the windowsill and the beautiful moldings around the frames. She closed her eyes and relived the moment, her hand touching the smooth moldings. She asked a single question with her mind, a simple *why*. Soon she was fast asleep with Mr. Jiggles cuddled next to her.

If she concentrated on something important prior to bed, she usually dreamed of it during the night. Answers came, sometimes unclear and ephemeral, other times more transparent. That night, she dreamt of a totally naked college-age man with red hair, fair skin, and freckles scattered across his cheeks.

He stood naked and cold next to the window that cracked and blew out. In the dream the window was also broken. Wind was blowing white curtains and rain through the opening and it pooled on the wood floors around his feet. The floors were shinier, with fewer dings, but the same. An old TV stood in the corner on the coffee table – the same one Ada had noticed earlier in the day by the couch. She looked at the TV carefully. It had two knobs in the front and a large set of rabbit ears, dating it definitively.

The red-headed man shivered and stared into her eyes but did not speak. He was tall, lanky, and remarkably muscled. One hand covered his manhood and the other wrapped across his body to clamp the bicep of the other arm as he shivered violently. His blue eyes burned into hers and all of his thoughts and feelings flowed into her mind like running water.

Ada felt the sensation of a loss so grievous it was unexplainable, along with an intense feeling of self-loathing coming from the man. The next set of feelings were a warning, the sense that something was terribly and horribly wrong, and that she should run from this place. From British Columbia. Live her life and forget her talents. Then he disappeared from her dream as quickly as he appeared.

Chapter Six: Overture

She woke the next morning to a chill in the air. The fire had burned itself out. The storm had finally passed, the power was on, and the sun streamed in through the windows. After fiddling with the thermostat, she made coffee and slipped into the bathroom. She looked up at herself in the mirror while she was brushing her teeth and noticed dark circles under eyes. It always seemed to wear her out when she had these dreams.

While she made breakfast, she charged her phone and texted Chris. The dream couldn't be explained over text or through a phone call, so she asked him to meet her for sushi by the bay for lunch. It was both exhilarating and terrifying to possibly find purpose in her special talents. She felt a buoyancy deep in her soul that was new.

After breakfast, she wandered into her room and began to look through the closet. She settled on a flowered dress and some black boots. Underneath the dress, she decided to wear peach silk panties and a simple bra-top camisole. She showered and tried to comb her crazy hair before deciding to let it air dry. She carefully applied mascara, some concealer, and lip balm to brighten her tired face.

When she finished getting ready, she poured another cup of coffee and sat down in front of her laptop. She did a few simple searches to see if any red-headed men had died in the 50's in Vancouver. She quickly discovered that was not a viable parameter for a search to find out more about the naked red-haired man. Furrowing her brow in frustration, she tried a few more things unsuccessfully. She would need Chris' help for sure. Together they might be able to figure more out.

She packed up her bag and pulled on a black-belted trench coat. She felt the heavy weight of her crazy hair bouncing down her back. It was springy, seeming to have taken on a life of its own in the humid post-rain air. She inhaled deeply, allowing the fresh air to wash over her. It smelled clean, scrubbed fresh by the rain since the storm had passed. With the sun out, it seemed like all the bad had been erased by the rain. She no longer felt so isolated. She no longer felt misunderstood. She had direction.

She drove out to the sushi place by the water and parked. She fed the meter with loose change and strolled down the street with her hands in her pockets, smelling the fresh salt air. She was early and had a little time to enjoy the water. She sat down on a bench on the pier and stared out at the sunny tranquility of the open water. A gull landed right next to her on the bench. He was staring at her quizzically, making her laugh.

How bizarre. The bird made a big show, trying to get her attention. He unfolded his wings and strutted around the bench, turning his head this way and that way, but always making eye contact. He stopped once she was staring back at him squarely, and the purest thought flowed through her from the gull. It was a sense of confidence. He was saying she was going to do this. She was going to return to the Boho Luna.

In shock she pondered whether she was feverish or losing her mind. *Since when did seagulls give their opinion on recent life events? Is he a gull or a life coach?* She held the back of her hand up to her forehead to check for a fever. The gull squinted at her and flew away towards the open water. Flustered, she got up, and made her way to the sushi bar. Just as she grabbed the handle of the door, she thought about Chris' great aunt and how she talked to animals. A big *ohhh* crossed her mind as the connection set in, making her pause for a moment before entering the sushi bar.

The inside of the restaurant was vibrant and bustling. She sat down near the hostess stand and waited for Chris. He walked through the door looking dapper as always, wearing a form-fitted black cashmere sweater and nice jeans. Ada stood up and smiled at him, her face glowing from the inside. They got a booth in the back away from the hustle and bustle of the lunch rush. The waitress brought them both water with lemon and they both ordered the special for that day, California rolls. As soon as the waitress was out of earshot, their conversation began. She was dying to tell Chris about her dream. She lowered her voice carefully and leaned in, just in case someone nearby might hear her and think she was an escapee from the mental health ward.

"I dreamt of a red-headed guy. He was about college-age, buff, and tall. He was totally naked. I have no idea why. I actually felt his feelings, but he didn't speak. He felt this profound sense of loss. He also warned that there was something terrible coming and he passed this feeling to me, that I should run away . . . leave. Escape."

Chris's eyebrows were raised so high they nearly disappeared in his hairline. He leaned closer and whispered. "Do you recognize him? Was anything familiar in the dream? I mean anything at all. Any small detail might help us."

Tapping her chin, she thought back carefully to some of the images from the dream. "Umm, I noticed a few things that might help us figure out who he is. There was an old TV that looked like it was from the 50's sitting on the old coffee table we saw when we were in the room. It was in front of the couch, like it was yesterday. Also, the floors were the same but shinier and in better condition.

She shook her head and realized they didn't have much to

go on. "From my past experiences with these dreams, I can say I'm quite sure this is one of the guys who died at the Boho Luna when it was a fraternity. That's all I could figure out, and I totally struck out searching the internet for deceased redheaded young men from Vancouver in the 50's.

"Oh, and one last detail. I do remember he had piercing blue eyes and was aware of his nakedness. He was covering his groin area and shivering violently as if he was cold. What do you make of it? How can we figure out who he is?"

She munched a California roll, drawing a blank on how to move forward with the mystery. This dream was as tricky as they came. They ate in silence for a while, wheels turning.

Chris' face lit up, and he raised up one finger mid bite, swallowing hastily. At that moment she saw an image of him as a little boy in grade school, raising his hand in class to answer a question, all but squirming out of his seat and saying, *ooooh! I know! I know!* He was wearing a blue button-down polo, like what they wore at private schools. Before she could ask him if he went to a private school as a child, he all but yelled out, making a couple nearby crane around and look at him. *Well, that was weird.*

"I have an idea. In the 50's most major events were chronicled in the newspapers. A death would always be in the paper, since it was the only way to spread information outside of gossip. There might still be people alive that knew our redheaded guy." He rubbed his chin in contemplation.

Ada interjected. "A guy with red hair alone, though, isn't that unusual. The only way someone who was at that fraternity during that timeframe might remember your dream guy is if there were scandal associated with that person. A suicide might be significant enough for someone to remember him. Off topic, but did you go to a private school as a child?"

He studied her quizzically for a moment before answering. "Why yes, yes I did. Did you have a dream or something?"

"I guess you could call it that. I was awake. it just happened. So weird. Something new every day."

She shook it off, deciding it was sort of low on the totem pole of weird things that had happened to them lately, and continued focusing on the red-haired man.

"I think the newspapers on microfiche at the downtown library is the quickest way to go. It's organized and can be searched electronically these days by keyword, so we might have some luck. I did have some success last night with researching the Boho Luna and I was able to determine the name of the fraternity, Kappa Beta Tau. So that will help give us a starting point."

"Wow, that's a great plan. Two heads are better than one. The library next, then?" she croaked out a bit weakly, still feeling drained.

"Ada, are you ok? You look really tired."

"I'm totally fine. Just need some fuel for our adventure and I'll be ready to rock and roll."

She smiled through her dark circles, that inner light still shining. Ada gobbled her meal with zeal. They ordered two strawberry shortcakes and coffee afterwards. The caffeine really perked her up and shook off some of the fatigue.

After Chris paid the tab, they walked outside into the bright but brisk day and headed to the library. It was just a few blocks, and they decided the walk would be good to drum up a few ideas.

CHAPTER SEVEN: CLARITY BEGINS

They walked up the library steps smiling and laughing. She took a moment to take in the beautiful building. Constructed from native stones and timbers, it looked to be hundreds of years old. She reached out and touched the ornately carved entry before entering. It felt bizarrely cold, making her wonder if the building had always been a library, or if it was haunted.

Soon after settling in at the microfiche machine, they hit pay dirt, and things quickly began to take an unexpected turn.

After searching for information on Kappa Beta Tao, they found a story with no photo about a young female college student named Kate Jones who ran through the glass windows on the second floor of the building. She died of exsanguination when a pane of glass sliced her throat as she was jumping. "We've got to find some photos, Chris. There's got to be a story with some pictures."

Chris shifted his bulky frame in the plastic library chair as he continued typing, his long, brown fingers flying over the keys. He almost looked comically too large for the small chair. Finally they found one. She sat transfixed staring at the screen. A newspaper clipping with a photo of a beautiful strawberry-blonde woman in a ball gown trimmed in satin filled the screen. Her lips were full and her smile spanned ear to ear. She was arm-in-arm with twin brothers in tuxedos, one on each side. Ada looked closer at the microfiche image, analyzing the details.

That was when it hit her. Before she could stop herself she

burst out with an *ah ha,* startling a young mother and her child who was a few stacks away. "Oh my god. There are two of him? Twins?"

"I'm not following you there, chief. Two of who?"

"The red-headed guy from my dream!!! I know it's black and white, but see all the freckles? This definitely looks like the same guy. Well, one of them is the same guy."

"Railroad Baron's Granddaughter Jumps out of 3rd Story Window after Apparent Mental Health Break," Chris read aloud. He continued to read the rest of the article.

. . . Stunning Vancouver socialite Kate Jones found dead Sunday morning after another macabre incident at the Kappa Beta Tao fraternity. She is pictured above with twins Gerald and Roger Fontenot at the winter gala for Dr. White's Orphanage.

"Well, she sure doesn't look glum or heavy-hearted in the photo. She looks vibrant, full of life. Look at the date, this was taken just weeks prior to her death. I'm printing this one, but let's keep looking." As they continued digging, they also found out that Kate Jones was engaged to one Gerald Fontenot, one of the redheads in the picture at the time.

When they searched for Gerald Fontenot, the results led them to several newspaper articles regarding his equally mysterious death, as well as his obituary.

Wealthy Socialite Kate Jones's Fiancé, Gerald Fontenot, Dies From Hypothermia at Kappa Beta Tao, said the article's headline. *Gerald was found in the third-floor bathtub of Kappa Beta Tao barely alive, completely naked and submerged up to his neck in ice-cold water. His death certificate listed hypothermia as the cause of death. Apparently his twin brother Roger Fontenot found him and reported that there was a roaring fire in the next room, which made the skim of ice in the bathwater impossible. Roger also stated Gerald was mumbling incoherently about his dead fiancé Kate Jones and a glowing ball before he was found in the tub.*

Chris read the last bit of the article out loud. *"This death is the most recent in a growing string of bizarre accidents at the fraternity. The president of the university could not be reached for comment, but the local archdiocese states an exorcism was performed after the bathtub incident."*

"Wonder if Roger Fontenot is still around? I'm sure he would have some insight about his brother's death. Let's search for Roger," Ada suggested.

The keys clicked away as Chris kept digging. The next item he found regarding Roger Fontenot was his death certificate. "Another dead end." Chris leaned back in his chair with his hands clasped behind his head.

Ada had an idea. She grabbed Chris's arm and almost jumped out of her seat. "Wait Chris, what if he married? Maybe we could find his obituary or a marriage announcement in the society section of the paper. These people seemed affluent—they would have posted photos and a wedding announcement in the paper. That was customary in this time period. You know, it was before social media."

Chris went back to searching.

"Obituaries, just three years ago. Says he was survived by his wife, a Delia Fontenot, formerly known as Delia White, and his brother-in-law, Mathias White," Chris shared. He appeared surprised.

Ada, however, was even more shocked. "Wait a minute, Delia is the elderly lady who lives in my building.

"She's a very decrepit white lady though, and our professor looks like he couldn't be a day past his fifties. Not to mention the fact that he's a black man. How could they be brother and sister?" Astonished, she shook her head.

The more they searched, the more questions seemed to come up. The growing mystery made her even more determined to solve it. "Let's look for the wedding announcement. Sometimes they share cutesy stuff like where they met. Maybe we'll find another clue. Let's switch seats. I'll take a turn."

They stood up, eager for some movement after hours at the microfiche machine. Ada gathered the articles she'd printed out and stowed them in a folder in her bag. They settled back in front of the microfiche machine, this time with Ada in the hot seat.

She got busy with the search and found what they were looking for in no time. "*Roger Fontenot and Delia White, married June 6th, 1956,*" Ada read the article out loud.

"Says here they met when Roger and his twin were volunteering at a fundraiser at Dr. White's Orphanage. Even though Mrs. Fontenot was plenty old enough to leave the nest, she must've stayed back to assist with the younger children. Makes more sense now with Mathias being her brother. They are adopted siblings, or children that never left Dr. White's orphanage."

"Since you live in the same building as Mrs. Fontenot, do you think she might meet with us to discuss the hauntings? Or what about Mathias, he might be more willing to discuss it with us?" asked Chris.

"Mathias might, it *is* sort of related to his course. Of course, then we'd have to fess up to *everything* that happened."

Chris visibly paled when she suggested telling their professor about meathead's threesome and their part in it.

She felt her own cheeks flush as her mind rambled through the idea of telling a perfect stranger about the scene they witnessed, too. Then they'd have to tell him about the blown-out windows as well. They'd both essentially strip their bizarre existence bare to a total stranger. *They're going to lock us away at the funny farm after this is over and throw away the key.* She held both temples and rested her head on the desk. Wracking her brain for a way forward.

"I have an idea, Chris. I think Mrs. Fontenot was probably closer to the situation, given that she married the surviving twin. Maybe we could arrange some sort of tea with them both? I assume they get along? Mrs. Fontenot is a bit of a pill, though. She is kind but also quirky. Then again, Mathias isn't exactly a typical professor. Did you see him bow in class? Or click his heals? Who does that?" Chris leaned back in his chair again studying the ceiling and mulling over her idea. He jumped forward with so much animation she nearly fell out of her own chair.

"I know what we can do. Tomorrow, we have the lecture at the Vogue. How about afterwards we invite Mathias to lunch at Boho Luna on Saturday? You could invite Mrs. Fontenot to come, too. We'll invite them under the premise that we are working on our class project and need their help. Even though you and I both know this is much more personal." Chris was smiling with lukewarm confidence.

Ade felt like he was right, this could work.

He continued with his plan. "If there are people out there with answers to why we are who we are and can explain why we do what we do, we need to find them. I mean, what if there's more that we can do and we are simply ignorant, and just learning to spread our wings? This is still going to be embarrassing for a lot of reasons, but I feel like this is the right thing to do."

"I definitely feel that way too, Chris. Things change and progress for me on a daily basis. It's very disconcerting to be so different, and it is an unending source of anxiety for me. I mean, I just can't continue my life like this, with no answers. If nothing else, it would be nice to ascertain if there are other people like us. It's changed my life meeting you and—I'm embarrassed to say this—but you are filling a void. I really needed a friend that I could share my strange life with! I was shocked to find someone just as unusual." She exhaled, feeling like she'd stripped herself bare to him.

Chris stared out the window, his expression stony and unreadable. As he turned to look back at her, the intensity in his gaze was almost palpable. "I have this feeling that Mathias definitely knows something." Chris tapped his notebook with the point of his pen decisively. "Maybe he teaches this class so he can find people like us. He could be teaching as a way to seek us out. We could be way off base, but I just don't think so. Sounds like we have a plan Ada. We have to do this. Just suck it up and do it." Chris started packing up his things. "We are done here. Let's go home so you can work on Mrs. Fontenot, and you look like you need some rest. We still need to research the Vogue as well before tomorrow's lecture."

Ada grabbed a few more printouts and slipped them into her folder. Hurrying back to her car in the crisp air, she still felt a lightness in her spirit that hadn't been there last week. *It feels good to have purpose. And the prospect of possibly having answers and direction feels even better.*

CHAPTER EIGHT: CHANGES

As Ada pulled up to her apartment, she pondered why she hadn't experienced much paranormal activity in her building. With the building's bleak past as a brothel, it was a good candidate for supernatural phenomenon to occur — certainly more than cold doorknobs and the smell of lilac. She sat in her car regarding the old apartment building and thinking about its past. Despite its history, her home still felt like a sanctuary.

As if sensing her presence from across the street, Mr. Jiggles appeared instantaneously in the window of her apartment. Ada watched her cat as he stared down at her with the brawn and arrogance of a full-sized lion surveying his kingdom. It made her think about the bizarre encounter she;d had with the seagull down by the water near the sushi bar. *Will I start reading Mr. Jiggles mind next? What will my fat little bastard have to say? Where's my tuna tartar?*

She smiled and shook her head as if that would wash away the strangeness of recent days. At least her apartment wasn't empty and lonely. Mr. Jiggles was always there waiting for his snack, plus snuggling with him was cathartic. She gathered her courage and got out of the car, walked quickly up the steps, and through the main door. No lilac smell greeted her. She checked her mailbox before scanning the hallway and running up the steps leading to her place. She sighed in relief once inside with the door locked and closed.

Mr. Jiggles meowed and purred, rubbing against her legs. like a normal cat. Nothing prophetic to say whatsoever. She sighed and dropped her backpack on the couch, feeling a little silly about her thoughts regarding Mr. Jiggles.

"Are you just here for the snacks and snuggles Mr. Jiggles?" She gave him an obligatory chin scratch as she headed toward the kitchen. A quick rummage through the fridge produced frozen pizza and a soda for dinner. She popped the pizza in the microwave, and her focus settled on the candlesticks Mrs. Fontenot had brought her when the power went out. It was the perfect reason to pop down to her apartment and ask her to lunch on Saturday at Boho Luna. The microwave hummed away. *I might have this task done before the microwave beeps.*

Grabbing the candlesticks, she slipped out the front door of her apartment and went down to Mrs. Fontenot's place. She knocked tentatively and waited patiently. Mrs. Fontenot didn't answer. She knocked again, this time a little louder.

After a couple minutes of silence, Ada heard a thud and a meow from the other side of Mrs. Fontenot's door. After some shuffling, the elderly lady finally appeared.

She looked sleepy in a surprisingly risqué black silk robe complete with ruffles around the collar that stood up against her tiny aging neck. She held a seal-point Himalayan cat with bright blue eyes under her arm. Mrs. Fontenot's own eyes were completely rimmed in some sort of purple night cream, giving her the appearance of a lavender-eyed raccoon. The cat regarded Ada with thinly veiled disdain. She had clearly interrupted their bedtime ritual. Feeling awkward and devious at the same time, she held out the candlesticks.

"Thank you so much, Mrs. Fontenot. These were so helpful. It can get scary up there during those bad storms. I don't know how you do it down here alone all the time. You must be lonely."

"No big deal, my dear! And, please, call me Delia. I'd invite you in for tea to catch up, but you caught Baxter and me as we were headed off to bed. If he doesn't get his beauty sleep, he can be really *catty*." She laughed at her own joke.

Ada noticed at that point that Mrs. Fontenot—Delia—was also not wearing her teeth. *Oh god. It's me in fifty years. Toothless with a feline bed partner.* She steeled herself and decided to get it over with. "Would you like to join my friend Chris and me for lunch Saturday, instead? We are working on a school project and thought you might have some insight. I know you've lived in Vancouver your entire life and must have seen a lot of events here firsthand." To her surprise, Delia's entire face lit up with delight.

"I would love to! Embarrassed to say it, my dear girl, but I've lived enough for five women, and I've seen as much, too." She began to puff her chest up proudly with her double-edged statement, eager to be included. It appeared she really did want to get out of her apartment.

"Perfect! See you at lunch time at Boho Luna. Well, I don't want to keep you, and I've got a pizza in the microwave oven."

Before Delia could protest and suggest a different venue, the fresh redhead from the second floor had turned and zipped back up the stairs. Delia felt her face begin to flush hot around her raccoon purple eye mask. She looked down at Baxter. He regarded her flustered state with indifference. As she turned to lock her apartment door, it dawned on her that Ada knew who she was. Already. She also realized that the young woman had tricked her quite adeptly, playing a crummy hand quite deftly.

If she already knows who I am, then she knows who Mathias is. How much has she actually figured out? She tapped her chin. *I bet that girl doesn't even know who or what she is. Let alone what Mathias and I are.* She padded into the kitchen in her black silk slippers and poured some sherry into an antique-leaded glass goblet. She plopped down at the side table, dropping Baxter onto her lap.

She sipped her drink thoughtfully while stroking his thick fur. With her free hand, she brandished the unique stone on the candlestick holder. *Does she know what this actually* is? *I bet not. One thing is for sure, this is going to be interesting.*

Ada's bolting retreat up the stairs left her breathless. She leaned her back against the closed door of her apartment and sighed in relief. Mr. Jiggles regarded her strange behavior with a puzzled meow. She checked on the pizza. It smelled delicious but wasn't quite done.

Her whole trip down to Delia's place had only taken a minute. She kicked off her shoes as she headed down the hallway, stripping along the way. She stopped to fiddle with the thermostat before heading into her bedroom for some warm fleece pajamas. *Not exactly sexy but oh so comfy* — the perfect ensemble for a night on the sofa researching the Vogue and cuddling with Mr. Jiggles.

After Ada changed into her pajamas, she took the pizza out of the microwave. The sight of the bubbling cheese made her realize she was ravenous. She decided to make a pot of coffee and mix in some Irish whiskey. It would help settle her nerves a bit so she could concentrate. She grabbed her plate and coffee and plopped down on the sofa with her laptop. After gobbling the food and doing a bit of preliminary research, she realized she hadn't even texted Chris yet to let him know how it went with Mrs. Fontenot. At that moment Mr. Jiggles decided to come over and knead his little paws on her chest. He stared at her while purring. Exhausted, she closed her eyes for just a moment. Sleep began to tug at the far corners of her mind as she thought about the day's events. Her body was worn out and she felt her mind slowly disconnect and give in.

Chapter Nine: Autumn surprises

Sunlight streaming through the windows, and Mr. Jiggles' obnoxiously loud purring startled her awake the next morning. She got up and stretched in the early morning light. Coffee was in order, and a quick jog around the neighborhood. She loved an exhilarating jog in the mornings. Running energized her and got her blood flowing. While the pot brewed, she put on her jogging clothes and gym shoes. She fed Mr. Jiggles and slipped out the front door.

The day was warmer than the previous one and shaping up to be beautiful. A strange thing happened a few blocks from her apartment as she was jogging. She met a man who appeared to still be drunk from the night before and had passed out in his car. He was stumbling out of the car he must have slept in when he partially blocked the sidewalk with a drunken stagger.

He was oblivious to her or the fact that he was out on a public street. He opened his fly and began peeing on a flowerpot in front of a pub. As she jogged past him, she smelled bourbon and recycled beer as well as the cloying scents of urine and body odor. As soon as she smelled him, an image of a woman in a hospital bed came to her, her body ravished by chemo. She was smiling and mouthed the words "Let me go . . . It's my time."

Profound feelings of loss and grief emanating from the drunk man flowed through her mind. An overwhelming sense of love enveloped her senses. She looked back at the drunken man to see his head tilted to the sky and the morning sun as tears rolled down his weathered cheeks. At that moment, Ada realized that the feelings of loss and grief and the image she saw belonged to the man. They were his experiences, his life.

As the realization hit her, Ada doubled over with her hands on her knees, catching her breath. She looked back at the entrance of the pub, but the man was gone. She decided to add some miles to her jog to clear her mind. Either she was totally losing it, or something else was going on. *Yesterday I thought a seagull was judging me. Today I think I'm reading some random drunk dude's mind. What's next! Weirder yet, who knew seagulls had opinions!*

She made it back to her apartment and poured herself some coffee with a shot of whiskey. As a rule she didn't typically drink before breakfast, but this week was something else. She kicked her shoes off and walked to her bedroom, intent on finding an outfit for the day. She decided on a plaid winter shirt over a tank top and a comfy pair of jeans with her beaten-down but comfy knee-high brown boots. Underneath it all, she decided to wear a pair of silk panties and a simple matching white silk bra. She headed into the bathroom and attempted to wash the events of the morning away. After quickly running a comb through her hair, she rubbed some rose oil over her dry skin. After dressing up, she decided to put on a little mascara and have more coffee spiked with alcohol.

She sat down next to Mr. Jiggles, sipping the hot brew when she realized she hadn't texted Chris about Mrs. Fonetenot. She quickly dropped him a note and let him know Mrs. Fontenot had taken the bait. She picked up her laptop and continued researching the Vogue. She had a calculus class prior to the lecture at the Vogue and needed to wrap up her homework.

Before she knew it, it was time to leave. She made a quick peanut butter sandwich and headed out the door.

Calculus class was as it always was — a bore. She weathered the academic rigor it demanded, but it was not her favorite class. Her mind wandered to the offsite lecture at the Vogue. She also pondered whether she would be able to make eye contact with meathead and his harem. The sound of the other students shuffling their notebooks and bags as they packed up brought her back to reality. Excited about the next class, she hurried to her car.

It was only a twenty-minute drive to the Vogue. She found a parking space in the historic district and realized she was a little early. Her phone hummed in her bag and she rifled around to locate it. It was Chris letting her know he was also already there. He'd already gone in and was waiting for her. The owner of the theatre happened to be at the front box office, and he'd told Chris to feel free to look around. She smiled. *Will we have more luck today on our quest for answers?*

She walked into the theatre and stopped, taken aback by the intact period details and architecture. The building was stunning, with an art deco theme. Original marble and carved stone covered the entry, floor to ceiling. It reminded her of something from a magazine. She felt a sort of electric excitement begin to pulse through her body.

She walked up to the ticket counter, smiling at the aging man on the other side. He had shortly cropped silver hair and crow's feet sprouting from the corner of his smiling eyes. She noticed he had the quintessential soft midsection of a middle-aged man and wore a designer button-down shirt that matched his icy blue eyes. He was also wearing just a hint of eyeliner.

"Have you seen a tall well-dressed black man?"

"You mean the chocolate god? About twenty-five? You could bounce a quarter off that ass. Firm." He gestured with his hands as if he was holding two ripe melons.

She felt her face flush hot and nodded her head politely but gave him a little side eye. He smiled at her, and she couldn't help but think he looked more devious when he smiled. There was something wolf-like about all of his super white teeth.

"I'm so sorry. I'm Michael, the owner. You've probably seen me on TV. Soap operas, a few movies."

He fluffed his hair at the back of his head, exactly how Ada had seen her grandmother do when her hair was short. His words resonated with her as forced nonchalance. It was as if he really wanted everyone to know of his *famousness*, but he grasped that people were tired of hearing about his soap opera and movie appearances. Finished preening, he rested his hands on his lap. He shrugged his shoulders up and beamed another effeminate but shark-like smile at Ada.

"He went that way, upstairs to the private boxes that over-look the stage. I told him to feel free to explore and look around. You know, I've known Mathias for years, and I love that he teaches his class here periodically. He's helped a few spirits find their . . . um . . . way out of here."

"It's that simple, then? Show them the door, burn a little sage, and poof?"

He threw his head back and laughed just a little too loudly. This time when he spoke there was an edge of sarcasm.

"Not exactly. It depends on who and what is hanging around. The good thing is much of what you are curious about will be discussed in Mathias's class — but in a sweeping generality sort of way."

There was an awkward pause after his last words. She got the impression that sweeping generality wasn't remotely what was going to happen in Mathias' class. The theatre owner almost seemed like he knew something but didn't know if he should give away his hand, like he was holding something back.

"Thanks." With that she turned and walked away. Michael's odd behavior left her with the feeling he wasn't going to elaborate much more about what happened in the theatre. In fact, she had the distinct feeling he was hiding something big, like a redhead-eating demon.

Ada eventually reached two grand staircases, curving to her left and to her right. She took the one to her right and slowly made her way up each step, admiring the stunning stone and art deco tilework. Her steps echoed through the theatre as she made her way upstairs.

When she made it to the top, she heard a conspiratorial *pssst*. She found Chris at the back of a long corridor. Doors leading to the theatres state-boxes — which offered a birds-eye view of the stage — were evenly-spaced along the left side of the hallway. He smiled broadly while putting one finger over his lips to shush her. She tip-toed her way toward him with eyes furrowed quizzically. *Oh god. What's going on now?*

He motioned for her to sit down in one of the plush red velvet seats of the box. She sat down and looked out across the cavernous theatre. There were tiered seats in the lower area and several floors of boxed suites along the sides. The theatre was totally dark with the exception of a spotlight focused on a small table and two chairs on the stage. Just then she heard familiar giggling below in the cheap seats — Dana and Kari. Their voices carried up as if they were right next to Chris and Ada — a quirk due to the way the theatre had been built. A hundred years ago there wouldn't have been sound systems.

Kari's high pitched voiced rang out with surprising clarity. She pointed at the table up on the stage as she spoke. Her gait was jaunty and loose as she walked down the aisle way. "Want to take bets? Kevin will want a good fuck right up there on the table — in the spotlight. Bets on how long he will last? I've got a twenty spot on less than five minutes."

Dana flanked her and laughed dryly before flipping her dark hair over her shoulder. Her husky guttural tones carried just as well to the upper box seats. "That's not a fair bet. We both have the same over under. I bet he lasts two minutes, and he makes that open mouth gawking face when he comes. He's such a pig, but such a good lay. Too bad men don't come with the whole package."

"I'd like to see him rail you, Dana, I mean, geez. When was the last time you had sex with a man? Heterosexual missionary sex. Beefy. Carnal."

"Oh, don't say women don't do carnal *or aggressive*. I've been with more than a few that were better than even Kevin. A good quick fuck would sure start this boring ass class out right though, that's for sure."

Dana looked around and tapped her lips, perplexed.

"I will say that since he prefers blondes — and we know he's going to be quick about this — you should probably hide."

"Why don't I go sit up on the table so when he gets here, we're ready to go? He only has one choice."

"Ok, I'm out."

Kari's blonde hair flounced over her shoulder and she slipped back out of the theatre.

Ada looked at Chris wide-eyed. Chris looked back at her with equal surprise and a devious smile. This time they had a choice about watching what was about to go down, and they decided to watch anyway.

They heard a heavy door slam, and in walked meathead. He sauntered down the center aisle of the cheap seats, focus locked on Dana, who sat on top of the table onstage. She sat with her long legs crossed, thigh high black heeled boots revealing about 12-inches of creamy white skin before her frayed jean skirt. She unbuttoned a faded flannel shirt as he walked towards her. He jumped onto the stage, reached out, and unsnapped the front clasp of her bra. Her breasts were large and slightly pendulous, her dark nipples standing out against the paleness of her skin. She pulled out the riding crop from her bag and slapped it against one hand. Her long dark hair was loose and wild around her shoulders, and she had a carnal look in her eyes. She looked him up and down like he was a piece of juicy steak.

"You're late, and you've been a bad, bad boy. If you can't make it up to me, I'm going to have to spank you. Whip that tight little quarterback ass. How hard can you fuck me, quarterback boy? Do you think I'll be a happy girl, or will you need a whipping?"

Meathead's eyes bore into Dana's. He ran his hands over both of her breasts and cupped them, pushing her legs apart with his knees. She unzipped his jeans and wrapped her hands around his large erect shaft. While stroking him, she pulled his pants down along with his boxers, so his bare ass was showing. Then she whipped him once, hard enough that the cracking sound rang out across the entire theatre, and he winced.

Ada could see tears in his eyes even from her vantage point.

Then Dana grabbed his head and buried it in the mound of dark curls between her legs while lying back, her wild brunette locks splayed out across the table.

"Eat me, and fuck me with your tongue until I'm ready, or I will make the next spanking count."

He looked up at her with surprise as he slid his tongue inside her vagina. She moaned with her eyes closed, digging her nails into his head. His cum dripped onto the floor of the stage.

As her moans escalated and sounded more frantic, he pushed his fully engorged cock into her. He started fucking her hard, sparing no mercy, making her cry out. Then he grabbed her hair. His gaze bore into hers as he pumped her, his expression emotionless. He continued to fuck her hard until she came in a gushing squirt and screamed his name.

Ada heard the wet splash up in the boxes.

He finished just after she did with a satisfied moan. Instead of collapsing on top of her in exhaustion, he pulled up his pants, zipped up, and walked away. He stopped at the edge of the stage and turned back to face her. She was sitting up looking dazed as she began snapping her bra back in place.

"Spank me again bitch, I'll make you pay. You got that? Don't damage the merchandise. The other ladies will notice.

'Whatever, you prick. Next time I'll get that other cheek, too. You're lucky you have a big ass cock, because you sure aren't the nicest guy I've ever met." She laughed at him so hard at that point she almost choked. She hopped off the stage and grabbed his arm.

"Where's Kari? I bet she has a purse flask. I need a little nip after *that*." He looked at her with mild disdain. "Fix your lipstick. You look like a harlot."

"I am a harlot."

They jabbed at each other all the way to the back of the cheap seats, where they plopped down.

Chris and Ada stared at each other, wide eyed over the entire exchange. Ada looked away from him and down at her shoes, shaking her head sheepishly, feeling a little like a voyeur. The entire encounter on stage had lasted less than five minutes.

Chapter Ten: Metamorphosis

The pair watched their classmates filter into the theatre, still stunned into silence. Then Mathias finally arrived. He walked down the aisle with the owner, deep in serious discussion. Their hushed words were muted but passionate. Chris and Ada decided to head downstairs and sat up front to be closer to Mathias and the lecture. The owner headed back up the aisle and shooed Kevin and his harem down to the front. He took out his laptop and began doing some work.

Ada looked at the time on her phone — they still had plenty of time before the lecture. She locked gazes with Chris, and in quiet understanding they decided it was time to rope Mathias into lunch with Delia. Chris cleared his throat as they approached their professor.

"Do you have a sec, Prof? Ada and I have a quick question."

"Absolutely, my Luminaries. What can I do for you?"

"We had some questions about the alleged hauntings at Boho Luna and thought maybe you could meet us for lunch there on Saturday . . . umm, around noonish? Also, so we don't blindside you, Mrs. Fontenot — Ada's neighbor — will be there. I think she's your sister?"

"Well. What a surprise! I would love to meet you there and my sister. That place has quite the storied past. I attended not just one, but two failed exorcisms sanctioned by the church there and multiple spiritual cleansings."

Chris and Ada glanced at each other wide eyed. Chris cleared his throat. To Ada's critical eye, Mathias' facial expression did not convey surprise.

"Ada and I had something happen on the second floor of the Boho Luna the other day. It was . . . um . . . bizarre?"

Chris' vagueness and the way he ended the statement as a question earned a slightly raised eyebrow from their professor. Ada discreetly elbowed Chris in the ribs, broke into the conversation, and changed the subject. She was anxious to prevent Chris from spilling the entire story to Mathias just yet. It was still very fresh and embarrassing.

Chris cocked his head sideways in mock surprise.

"I hope your sister's attendance won't be a problem. She has so much knowledge of the history of the area, I thought it would be great if she came." Ada was eager for reassurance that she hadn't offended Mathias, especially after the stunt she'd pulled with his sister.

"Certainly not! I'm sure she will love the opportunity to get out and wear her fancy shoes and outfits. She still dresses like she's a swinging sixty-five, pun intended."

They all began laughing, Mathias the loudest. Ada could not shake the sense that Mathias had fully expected them to bring up his sister. He was not remotely surprised that Ada was his sister's neighbor or that she would be attending lunch with his students. Questions flew through Ada's mind like rapid fire. She was unable to slow the stream of unending questions Mathias' odd responses generated in her mind. Have *they already connected the dots? Nonsense, how could they connect dots I can't even connect? Unless they know about everything already. Do they know more about me than I do?*

When they returned to their seats, Mathias began his lecture about hauntings and the various theories to date. He recounted the assorted incidents at the theatre as examples of the various theories.

His voice became a low hum as Chris and Ada traded texts. Both were feeling ill at ease. After an hour, he opened the floor up for discussion and personal stories. Nearly every student had a question or personal experience to share, although none were quite like Ada and Chris' experiences.

As the students filtered out at the end of the class, the owner made his way back up to the stage. He stood with his hands on his hips, looking indignant. Clearly the earlier discussion he'd had with Mathias was still weighing on him. Chris and Ada sat glued to their seats as they eavesdropped.

"Mathias, can we go back to the ladies dressing room? The scene of all the never-ending sightings. I've had the building blessed and cleansed many times, but one sad sack keeps coming back. The plumber and I were working back there a few weeks ago and both of us heard her weeping."

Mathias' arms were crossed firmly across his chest as he shook his head in annoyance.

"Ok, Michael. I'll hear you out. I'm sure it's probably hard to keep the business running if patrons and actors think it's cursed or haunted. It never ceases to amaze me what garbage people believe is real compared to what they dismiss."

Michael moved closer to Mathias closing the gap between them. He lowered his voice and leaned in before speaking discreetly. "I have no idea what is going on or why she's back, but I can't have her playing games with the actors while they are getting ready back there. She's done some devious things over the years, and I want her out." Michael paused when he caught Ada and Chris eavesdropping. "Mary, I would love for you and your wingman to come, too."

Ada felt confusion spread across her face.

"Umm, I'm not Mary. My name is Ada."

"Oh, *sure* it is. Ada this time. Got it. Check."

Here we go. Cue the circus music.

Mathias had a stony expression on his face. With his head down deep in thought, the professor rummaged through his bag. He brought out a candle and a candlestick holder like the one his sister had loaned to Ada the night of the storm. The candle itself looked homemade, with bits of herbs and lilac flowers suspended in a translucent lilac-colored wax. Ada spoke up. "Your sister has the same candlestick holder. Is that hematite?"

"Yes, a unique variety found in a certain place in Canada. This candle is made from sage and lilac soaked in holy water. It smells a bit like a bouquet in a sausage factory but it does occasionally work to banish a stubborn spirit."

Ada raised a brow. "That's interesting." *So, Mathias knows how to expel spirits. I wonder what else he knows.* She pressed on, peppering him with more questions. "In the spirit of our coursework, prof, can you give us any background about this weeping woman in the dressing room? Who is she? And why can't she move on?"

"I'm glad you asked, Ada. Years ago, an actress named Imogene became pregnant with a very famous *and very married* railroad baron's love child. Imogene was beautiful — inside and out — and she was loved by the community. She was super talented, too. She became despondent when the baron suggested Imogene let his wife raise the baby. His wife was infertile, and Imogene was an unmarried actress, so of course he thought it was a good arrangement. He'd have his child to raise, his wife would be happy, but he clearly wasn't considering Imogene.

"As the story goes, she committed suicide in the dressing room shortly after giving birth to baby Eugene, but since there were no witnesses, it's only conjecture. She always appears and seems to have something to say, but she's unaware that she's dead or that the baron is dead. She has no idea how much time has passed."

Michael cleared his throat overly dramatically and interjected. "Ahem. The baron's infertile wife, Vivian, was active in the theatre and found Imogene's body, leading to the speculation that it was a murder. To add to the theory it wasn't a suicide, Vivian took the baby, baby Eugene, home the very day of his mother's death. The maid at the baron's home said they had a fully decorated nursery for a baby boy all ready to go, as if they were expecting him. To further complicate things, the baron gave Eugene the very same theatre his mother died in when he was an adult."

She looked deeply into Michael's eyes. There was something else going on that he wasn't addressing. She just knew it. Deep down. He now looked weary, and some of the fire was missing from his bright blue eyes. "So Michael, do you mind telling us how you came by the theatre? I mean, you are a famous actor and Vancouver is lovely, but I can't imagine anyone would randomly buy a theatre in Vancouver. Especially if they were a well-known actor. Unless of course, they had a connection to Vancouver."

"The truth is, Ada, I am Eugene's great grandson. I am also the second cousin of one of your classmates. Do you happen to know a Kevin?"

She was floored by the revelation.

"Oh boy, do we all know a Kevin."

He laughed dryly and paused just a second too long. "Yeah, that kid's dad. Wow. Such a dark soul. I caught him and his brother at about middle school age backstage during a Christmas pageant assaulting another student. One was sitting on top of another kid literally strangling him, and the other one was laughing while the kid turned blue. It was the one with that blank looking expression doing the strangling. I tackled him and kicked them both out. You can imagine how that went over in the family." Michaels face flashed red as he recalled the memory.

Ada locked eyes with Chris as things slowly started to make more sense.

"So it could have been the baron, his wife, or both of them that killed Imogene. Birds of a feather, they all kind of sound awful." Chris speculated, shrugging his shoulders.

Mathias spoke up. "This is not so easy to solve. If it had been them, Imogene would have been heartbroken with grief, but she seems confused. It could have also been the baron's assistant, Garrett. Rumor has it Garrett did the baron's dirty work, his *heavy lifting*. I've seen some old photos, Garrett looks like a short man, stoutly built with small cold eyes. The photos were grainy and black and white, so I couldn't discern much else. But I'll tell you, just looking at him sort of sends a shiver down deep into your soul."

Michael let out an exasperated sigh and stamped his foot. His arms were firmly crossed across his chest, and annoyance showed in every inch of his body.

"Not to sound insensitive, but great Grandma Imogene is getting on my last one. I've talked to her and talked to her. Can't get through. She just doesn't hear me. We've got to get down to business. I have a theatre to run, people! I've got actors arriving for rehearsal any minute," said Michael, impatiently. "Let's go, Mary."

"It's Ada." Chris corrected Michael a little more sharply than he expected.

Michael looked down sheepishly, hanging his head. He looked back up at Ada, smiling. "Yes, so sorry. Let's get moving." His smile and tone made the apology meaningless.

Mathias glared at Michael with cold disdain and shook his head. Ada watched the exchange with confusion. Her annoyance was building regarding their inside joke about this *Mary* person or whoever, and she was going to get to the bottom of that.

Mathias led the group backstage down a dark, dingy hall. The air seemed twenty degrees cooler and damper. The smell of mold, mildew, and cigars hung heavy in the damp air. About midway down the hallway, her sensitive ears picked up a very faint sound of whimpering. As they walked further down the hall, the cloying smell of cigars grew thicker and the whimper was now a wail. Feelings of inconsolable grief and loss permeated her mind, along with an unmeasurable hatred. It was strangely inexplicable, as she'd never experienced anything quite like it. The group kept moving forward as the sound of agony grew clearer and louder. At the end of the hallway, the dressing room's light was turned on and the door was wide open. Mathias took out a book of matches and prepared to light the candle as they neared the open door. Once Mathias lit the candle, she saw a shadow on the back wall of a woman in a long gown. Her head was down, and a cascade of wild hair rioted down her back as she continued to weep. Her cries were deafening. The group closed in on the apparition with leery caution. The wailing Imogene's head jerked up as they entered the room. She was oblivious to Mathias's special candle.

"Mary, Mary. Is that you? I knew you would come. You can help me. He did this. He—he—he did this to me. Where is my baby Eugene?"

She stuttered the last words out between choking sobs, shrieking out Eugene's name with the fury only an angry mother could muster. Mathias looked at Ada and made a shushing motion with his finger. He cleared his throat and began speaking in a very calm and deliberate manner.

"Imogene, we know he did it. He is long gone now though, and there's nothing to be done. Mary can't find him. She can't help you. She isn't ready. You need to be at peace. Please go and rest, Imogene."

The candle blew out as an icy blast of air hit the group. Sucking in his breath in surprise, Mathias lit a match and relit the candle. The figure's wails turned into a shrill shriek.

"Please help me. I can't believe no one will help me. I'm going to make him pay!"

"Not today. Maybe another day. I think he's already paid up."

Ada moved closer to Mathias. He shook his head and gestured silently for her to keep quiet. Ada realized the feelings of grief that flooded her were Imogene's pain. It felt like it was her own burden to bear, and she could not heed Mathias' warning.

Ada began to speak calmly to the apparition. "Imogene. It's Mary. Can you tell me what happened?"

Imogene's sobs lessened, and she began to speak with more clarity.

"I was breast feeding baby Eugene in between scenes of the Friday matinee. He was a ravishingly hungry baby. A growing boy. The man — he was in my dressing room. I didn't know." She began sobbing again.

An image of a beautiful fresh-faced woman holding a chubby baby boy as he suckled hungrily on her breast came to Ada but was gone as soon as it appeared.

"You can do it, Imogene. I need to know more of what happened, or show me, for baby Eugene's sake."

The sobs tapered off and she disappeared. Just then a large standing dressing mirror began to tilt slowly forward. The antique wood creaked audibly as if someone were leaning on it before it crashed forward, shattering glass into a thousand pieces. Mathias and Ada jumped backwards just as it fell, missing them both by a few feet. Color rose on Ada's cheeks, and she realized she was no longer scared but angry.

"Imogene, that's it," Ada said firmly. "If you aren't nice to the living, I will not help you. I know something about baby Eugene. If you want to know what's going on, you are going to behave. Got it?"

The cloying scent of cigars suddenly seemed stronger in the room and the candle was blown out again. The temperature was rising back to normal.

Mathias lit the candle again, and they backed slowly out of the room. The smells of sage and an undertone of lilac filled the room. It was all over before it started. The smells of cigars dissipated. Nothing remained but a dimly lit dressing room, and a hall that smelled of a hundred years of musty air. Mathias turned on the lights of the vanity, further illuminating the room and making it hard for any shadows to peek through. He mumbled a chant under his breath, too quiet for anyone to make out, and sprinkled crumbled herbs around the periphery of the room.

"Well, that's it. She's gone."

"You mean she's gone, *again*. As in, someone who comes and goes. Also, I told you her name was Mary. It *is* Mary. As in *the* Mary." Michael made an extravagant and frustrated hand gesture in Ada's direction, nearly poking her in the face.

Ada jerked her face out of range, feeling more confused now than the first time he'd called her Mary. "Look, I don't know what that shadow lady's problem is, but my name *isn't Mary*." Ada felt herself flush. Her words came out angrier than she'd expected. As soon as she stopped speaking, the bulbs around the dressing table began to burn out one at a time.

With that Mathias dispatched everyone down the hall. "That's it, everyone. I have work to finish in here without you three making it harder. Chris and Ada, I will see you tomorrow for lunch with Delia. We can talk more then."

Michael huffed off down the hallway. His anger-fueled steps propelled him out of sight in seconds.

Eager to leave the creepy hallway, Ada and Chris followed suit and didn't slow down until they were outside in the fresh air. Exhausted, Ada was craving a bit of peace and quiet at her apartment. Eyes closed, she rubbed her temples in the warmth of the setting sun. "Chris, it's getting late. I've still got some homework to get done. I'll see you tomorrow at Boho Luna."

"Wait a minute, Ada. Aren't you the least bit surprised

about what we just saw? I mean, I've had a few odd things happen in my day — or I wouldn't be taking this class — but this takes the cake."

"I've had a few things happen that were pretty strange. Things you and I haven't discussed yet. However, I agree with you what happened in *there* takes the cake. I'm feeling a little overwhelmed, and I — I just need to process all this. I am exhausted, for some reason."

She fiddled through her purse for her car keys, feeling as shaken as she'd been in Boho Luna. Her hands jittered and shook as she rifled through her bag. "The odd things in my life have been escalating rather than de-escalating, and this is just one more crazy thing I can't explain. Just like you, events like these are the reason why I'm taking this class."

Chris was silent for a minute.

Ada sighed. "I'm sorry, I didn't mean to come across as being rude or frigid."

"It's okay, Ada. I understand. You know, one thing is for sure, Mathias knows something more than he's letting on."

Ada nodded. "Tomorrow I say we push him to come clean."

"I agree. Right now, though, I could use some time to decompress. A beer and binge-watching my favorite series sounds nice. What do you think?"

Ada stared deep into his warm brown eyes, then stepped forward and hugged him. The hug felt like she was hugging a brother or sibling.

"It does sound good. A warm fire and my cat. Some mindless Zombie TV."

She walked away towards her car looking over her shoulder and smiled back at him. Any bystander would have thought she was flirting. There was a degree of familiarity that anyone watching would notice. Though they were not attracted to each other sexually, they inexplicably had a sense of knowing each other well that belied the truth that they'd just met a few days prior.

CHAPTER ELEVEN: EVOLUTION

Before heading home, Ada ordered some food at the local Italian restaurant to go and bought a bottle of her favorite Chardonnay at the liquor store. With the delicious aroma of her dinner filling the car, Ada pulled up at her place already feeling less concerned about the day. Mr. Jiggles sat in the front window with his face pressed against the glass as if he knew she had ordered shrimp and alfredo sauce. She hurried from the car to the door away from the chilly air. She checked her mailbox and headed up to her room, eager for a glass of wine and a good meal. She was looking forward to some time spent not thinking of the day's events.

Her apartment was cold when she entered, so she threw some wood into the fireplace and lit it. Mr. Jiggles twirled around her legs, meowing and demanding a meal. She fed him some dry food topped with some of her shrimp alfredo and poured herself a glass of wine. She sat on the floor in front of the fire to eat her meal while she binged on Zombie TV.

She let her mind wander, thinking back to when her parents were still alive. She remembered her mother's warm smile on a summer day, watching nearby while Ada played in her sandbox — her tiny chubby hands in the warm sand. She wondered if Mathias could shed light on who her mother was when she was alive. Her grandmother always said Ada was like her mother. She suspected deep down all of this was connected.

She looked around to see Mr. Jiggles regarding her suspiciously from his perch on the coffee table. She placed her half-eaten plate next to him and watched him lick the plate clean after gobbling the remaining food. She poured herself one more glass of wine before switching off the TV. She changed into her pajamas and drank the glass of wine in bed. Before she knew it, she was fast asleep with Mr. Jiggles.

She woke up to another crisp fall morning with rays of warm sun streaming through the windows. She brewed up a pot of strong coffee and made some toast with fresh marmalade from the farmers market down by the docks. She fed the insistent Mr. Jiggles and poured some coffee. She went back to her room and carefully picked out an outfit that Mrs. Fontenot would find appropriate for an outing. She finally settled on a tea length flowered dress and a nice collared blouse, with a pair of conservative Mary Jane heels.

She took a shower, applied rose oil to every nook and cranny, then applied her makeup. She blew her hair dry and put it up on top of her head fastening it with her grandmother's antique hair clip. As she pinned up her hair, Ada remembered her mother doing the same thing when she was a child, with the same clip. These days Ada was thinking of her mother more often. A shiver went down her spine. For a moment, it almost felt like her mother was in the room with her.

It was a new feeling, the there-but-not-truly-present sensation. It was as if her mother was there guiding her or passing judgement on her choices. Using her small compact to view the back of her head, she looked at the brass clip holding her hair together. The bronze clip almost blended in with her coppery hair. Satisfied, she walked out of the bathroom and gathered her things. She felt both eager and weary at the same time for the lunch with Chris, Mathias, and Mrs. Fontenot.

She walked out into the crisp fall air and to her car. Her trip to Boho Luna was uneventful, and she texted Chris as soon as she arrived. He was already there having a beer at the bar. *A little liquid courage, as they say.*

She walked into Boho Luna, and a strange hush spread across the room when she walked in. A rather rotund bald man seated with his equally plump wife did a double take, his eyes openly appraising her from top to bottom.

Embarrassed, she blushed and put her head down, walking quickly to where Chris was seated at the bar. The patrons returned to their conversations and drinks, and the steady hum returned.

Chris flagged down the bartender, an elderly gentleman with salt and pepper hair and a chiseled face. "Can I get a Chardonnay for the lady, please?"

The barkeep brought the wine over, his eyes leveling with Ada's. They were a bizarre pale caramel, which she'd begun to equate with people like her and Chris. His eyes were almost exactly the color of Chris' eyes. An unspoken acknowledgement passed between the three of them as he handed her the glass wine.

"On the house, sir. Let me get you a shot of bourbon to back that beer, on the house as well. I have a feeling it's going to be an eventful day for the two of you."

Chris and Ada stared at each other, both their eyes wide in anticipation. Questions about the bartender were swirling through their minds as well. So many years of confusion coupled with big changes in their own bodies and minds was creating mounting anxiety.

"Milady, how 'bout a bit of top shelf tequila? Just a shot. On the house as well. My name's Gregory, by the way. I'm one of the owners here."

The faintest Irish accent rose to the surface, and Gregory sounded more like Greg-o-rah. Despite his calm demeanor, she sensed that the old man was also ever so slightly rattled. She had an overwhelming feeling that something ominous was about to happen. The bartender even poured a few extra shots of bourbon for himself.

"Whoa man, don't you need to chase that with something?" Chris smiled at the aging Irishman as he ribbed him.

"I'm an old Irish asshole. I could drink paint thinner and smile. I think my mum started putting Irish whiskey in my bottle when I was just a wee one. Chasers are for Americans."

He laughed and poured another shot and downed it.

"It will be nice to see Mathias and Delia. We've history. I guess you could call it that."

Chris and Ada looked at each other. They hadn't said a word to Gregory about Mathias and Delia. It was like he had read their minds. *Does Gregory have a special talent? Like mind reading?*

Ada eyed the decanter her tequila had come from. It was not in a normal tequila bottle, but an odd round crystal bottle with a long slim neck and a matching crystal stopper.

"That is a lovely decanter. Can I see it?"

He handed it to Ada, and she ran her delicate hands over the glinting cut crystal. Rainbows of light caught in each angle with light and rainbows dancing across the bar. He laughed again, and this time it had a crazy edge to it that wasn't entirely pleasant.

Taking a moment to eye Gregory after his creepy laugh, she sat the decanter back down, pinched her nose, and downed her shot, following it with a swig of Chardonnay. Chris followed suit and Gregory gave them all another round of shots. After about fifteen minutes the edge was gone on her frayed nerves. *Here goes nothing.*

Chapter Twelve: Old Friends Meet Again

Gregory's gaze shifted to the front entrance, and Ada turned to see if Mathias had finally arrived. Sure enough, Delia Fontenot was walking in through the door that Mathias dutifully held open. She smiled at him graciously as he held the door open, as if she didn't expect anyone to make such a chivalrous offer. She was wearing a black velvet fitted dress, with a loose fitting knit cape and a pair of black lace ballet slippers over black panty hose. Her crown of gray hair was adorned with a vintage black fascinator, complete with a black mesh veil that covered one eye. The fascinator had several large black feathers and a large black satin rose. She had a small and simple black handbag on her arm and wore bright red lipstick. As always, she walked with a cat-like grace that belied her age. She held Mathias' arm as he walked her to the bar and seated her next to Ada. In stark contrast to his sister's panache, Mathias was dressed very humbly in a gray sweater and slacks. Gregory wasted no time in anxiously demonstrating his hospitality yet again.

"Lady White, it's been a long time. Let me pour you some of that smooth Canadian whiskey."

"You remembered. On ice, doll. Make it a double, and one for my brother as well, but with club soda instead of ice."

Then the elderly woman leveled her gaze on Chris. Hawk-eyed, she appraised him carefully head to toe before addressing him. "Delia. Please to meet you." She presented her hand to him as if she was expecting him to kiss it.

Chris took the bait, held her hand and gave it an awkward peck on the back. With all the introductions in order, Delia grabbed Ada's arm with her claw like arthritis withered hand and smiled warmly.

As soon as Mrs. Fontenot touched her, a vision of a much younger Delia came to her, with the same red lipstick, a similar fascinator, a different bar. A much younger Gregory was also in the vision tending bar. Almost as soon as that vision came to her, a second one appeared to her in a short replay. It was Gregory fucking Delia in the back room of the bar. He pressed her up against the wall and seemed to expel months of pent up frustration in a carnal encounter. She could smell her perfume. She felt his desire. She felt Delia's orgasm, and saw the bartender tuck coins into her purse. The vision ended in a flash, almost over before it started.

She jerked her head towards Delia, then towards Chris to see if he had the same vision or daydream. Their gazes locked, and clear as day Ada heard Chris' voice in her head exclaiming *Delia used to be a prostitute!* At that moment, it all came together for Ada and she shared her realization with Chris telepathically. *Delia and I live in a building that used to be a brothel. How old is she? 200 years old? Why does Gregory look younger? Since when do we have telepathic conversations?*

Chris raised his eyebrows and shook his head. He pushed her Chardonnay towards her. Delia was smiling, seemingly basking in the past memory of her and Gregory. Her eyes were closed, and she drank the drink Gregory had brought her in what seemed like a single swig. When she placed her glass back down and opened her eyes, there was another drink in front of her. She turned her head and looked into Ada's eyes still smiling. It was very clear that the older woman had indeed been a prostitute at one time, *and* she didn't hate her former profession, either.

Mathias pulled up a stool next to the group. He was

smiling with a Cheshire cat-like intensity that only added to Ada and Chris' unease. Gregory poured Mathias a drink as his expression grew serious. He took a single calculated sip and began to speak with all eyes on him.

Ada couldn't help but notice that Mathias did not seem as remotely rattled as anyone else in their little group of kindred folk. *Is that what we are, kindred folk? Or just a bunch of batshit crazies headed for the mental health ward?*

Wasting no more time, their professor began to speak. "Well. Just as I suspected, my two Luminaries. You two are always the same, but always different — in every reincarnation. Century after century, different but exactly the same. Clearly you two have figured a few things out, or we wouldn't all be gathered here together. I mean, I'm quite sure we aren't all here to wax poetically about days gone by and to tell inflated ghost stories."

Mathias took a long sip of his bourbon, taking his time to roll the flavors over his palate. He turned his glass, tipping the bourbon around and around in a circle. His caramel eyes were so close to the amber of the liquid in the glass.

Ada's foot began to tap in an effort to diffuse her anxiety before it boiled over and she lost her nerve. But it was too late now. She needed to know what Mathias had to say, no matter how bizarre it seemed. She looked over at Chris. His lips were tense, his beautiful face marred with concern mirroring her own.

Mathias knocked back the last of his drink. "You and Chris are probably confused about what's going on and who you are. And Rightfully so."

He kept talking as Gregory poured him another drink. "Things are clearly starting to happen to both of you that are disconcerting at best. I hate to break it to you, but it's all about to get more bizarre, more dangerous. Essentially, whatever has already happened is just the beginning."

Mathias took a deep breath and looked away from them as

he took a sip of his drink. The bartender made a flourishing hand gesture in an effort to move the conversation along.

"Just tell them, Mathias."

Their professor cocked his head and sipped his drink silently. He was clearly less rattled than Gregory. Ada looked to Delia, who sat just as quiet as Mathias, not a bit nervous.

"Get on with it." Gregory waved his hand again. He seemed exasperated, like this was all old to him, as if people came in everyday that talked to the dead. "Either they believe it or not. Regardless, life is about to get odder for them both. We all know that to be true. The question is just how weird is it going to get? There's no way for us to know the answer to that question. At least not yet anyway."

He looked at his sister, taking a second to absorb her response to Gregory's outburst. Delia had a broad, proud smile across her weathered face.

Mathias held his hands out in front of him, clasping them together. He cracked his knuckles and stared at Gregory a second too long, reminding him who was in charge. Not a peep was heard from Delia, Chris, or Ada.

"Throughout history there have been certain people who keep humanity on track. Some of these people were rumored to have extraordinary talents. By extraordinary talents, I mean things along the lines of what you are both probably experiencing and more. In fact, so much more."

Mathias downed another drink.

"It's hard for me to even explain. Truth be told, I'm not even sure what either of you are capable of. It could be limited to mind reading and speaking to the dead. *Or*, you could be capable of much more, such as real-time slow-mos, talking to animals, or even visions of the future."

Delia interjected, her voice husky with the booze.

"My dear brother, don't forget the most important part—*extraneous sexual talents.*"

Gregory crossed his arms, disgust written on his face. Mathias began laughing so hard he choked on his drink. "There's more to life than sexual prowess, Delia. What if one of them is a Demi-god? An Arch Lumen? One or both of them could control minds, read minds, or pull evil out of mortal souls."

Mathias sipped his drink some more and looked at his Luminaries. Ada's cheeks were flushed, and Chris' eyes were rounder than usual.

"Let's back up a bit and start at the beginning. Number one, reincarnation is real. For example, a few Luminaries believe that you, Ada, are the reincarnation or a descendent of Mary Magdalene. For the record, I believe they are right. Your talents will help us figure out which one you are—a descendent or reincarnation."

"Oh, and by the way, there is a network of humans who are aware of us as well. They carry a small percentage of Luminary DNA, who had ancestors who were what we call halflings. We will get to halflings later. Michael, for example, is mostly human and he is indeed aware of us. Which is why he called you Mary, Ada."

Ada and Chris sat still in their stools dumbfounded but continued to listen attentively.

"Number two, we don't age the same way humans age. I have been about forty-five years old for over five-hundred years, so if you've found it odd that I look a little younger than Delia, it *is* odd."

His two new Luminaries seemed unable to speak. Mathias downed his glass and Gregory poured him yet another. Before continuing, he looked around the bar to confirm no other patrons were on the premises. He locked gazes with the bartender, then walked over to the door to put the *closed* sign up. With one last glance outside, he locked the doors, the old brass clicking into place with finality.

"Let's discuss the *odd* people like us. There's an entire community and classification system. So as not to overwhelm you, we will cover basic guidelines for extraneous talent levels. I myself am still learning things daily even after five hundred years. To further complicate this, talents can change and evolve as time passes. I'm assuming you two are beginning to experience these evolutionary talents, where one day you wake up and think you've mastered something but then it changes . . . evolves."

He got up and began pacing as he explained what was happening to his two newest students. The movement helped his thoughts flow as he worked out in his mind how to convey what he suspected was happening.

"There is a central energy that is in charge of all of us. We are all mentally, spiritually, and physically connected to this energy. It has come to be known as Ahm. Throughout history, Ahm has been called a number of things, but most typically, this energy is depicted as a god or goddess. Almost every organized religion can be traced and linked either directly or indirectly to Ahm. Every culture has a different name for Ahm, but it's all actually the same God." He stopped and looked at Chris and Ada, attempting to ascertain how confused he might have just made them. They appeared bewildered and maybe even a bit curious, but not angry. *A good sign. If they weren't what I think they are, they wouldn't be so open minded.*

Ada looked at Chris, whose eyes were as wide as hers. He seemed to be compulsively nursing his beer as if it was tethered to him and to the last shred of normalcy in life as he'd known it.

Mathias continued on. "Under Ahm are the Luminaries, and below them the Serfs. Ada, Chris, and I are Luminaries. We are considered Luminaries or leaders because we have the strongest talents of everyone. A Luminary, by definition, is a body or object that gives light, or a leader. There are different types of Luminaries."

Ada took a large swig of her drink and decided to speak up.

"Uh—Mathias, I don't feel like a leader. I am an anxious, fearful person. I mean, right now I don't think they would put me in charge of the deep fryer at the Burger Max on the corner."

A deep rumbling laugh began to bubble up from Delia. followed by Gregory and even Mathias. The old woman slapped her wrinkly hand on the bar and wiped tears from the corners of her eyes before she began to speak.

"My dear girl you don't have to feel strong *to be strong*. It's all about what talents you were blessed with and mastering them. Great strength among the Luminaries can come in an unexpected package."

His expression sobering, Gregory interjected. "She's correct. For instance, Delia smothered a serial killer in 1892 in this very building. I got him good and liquored up, Delia took him upstairs along with another girl under the ruse of a threesome. While the other girl gave him a blow job, Delia stood behind him massaging his shoulders. Just as he closed his eyes for the big finish, Delia covered his mouth and nose with rag soaked in chloroform. She then cradled his head in her ample bosom and pinched his mouth and nose shut. He was dead in a matter of minutes. When I found him, he still had a hard-on."

Mrs. Fontenot smiled deviously. "That being said, Gregory and I are only Serfs. Very talented, but not Luminaries. I am quite masterful at using sex to distract and to get things done. Gregory can occasionally read minds. But as you can see, neither Gregory nor I are as remarkable as either of you. Not in appearance or in talent."

Delia made a big show of adjusting her murderous bosom after explaining. Gregory eyed it lustfully, appearing completely unashamed at being attracted to a woman so much his senior.

"Your appearance means something. I mean, do you two think that people just naturally look like you two? Your appearance is a weapon, just like mine once was." A sly smile slid across her weathered faced.

Mathias continued with his lesson in the supernatural. "I am known as a teacher or headmaster of the young Luminaries. I identify young people and children who are blessed with extra talents and help them control and develop their gifts. Many times people like us are orphaned and I take care of them as a father would his children."

Chris and Ada turned and looked at each other, the wheels turning for so many coincidences, such as the orphanage and the fact that Mathias and Delia were brother and sister, although one was an aging white lady and one was clearly a black man.

Chris spoke up. "We were right, Ada." At the rest of the group's puzzled looks, he explained, "We figured Mathias chose to teach a course at the at the University that would help him identify people like us — or I guess *Luminaries,* as you call them, Mathias."

Ada thought out loud, "I bet most Luminaries are looking for answers, especially if their parents died, like ours, and they were raised by normal people. Maybe even Luminaries born to Serf parents are looking for guidance."

Mathias' somewhat somber demeanor darkened. "That brings me to my next point. This is not all fun and games. I must warn you, a number of us have violently died over the years at the hands of people who are our exact opposite, led by an entity I have come to describe as simply the Overlord."

Gregory began digging around under the counter, clinking bottles loudly. Mathias' voice again filled the room with his lecture. Ada stared at him rapt with attention.

"We have our talents for a purpose, namely, to keep everyone else safe. Over the last five hundred years, the Overlord has never ceased to amaze me. He has a penchant for death and destruction that defies reason. His means of enacting his vile purposes vary. There are foot soldiers on both sides. Our kind are the Serfs. There is no name for a Serf's equivalent on the other side, mostly because even average people without talents can be infected by the Overlord."

"I hate to interrupt, but could I have a cheese plate, please, my dear: Maybe some fruit and crackers? All this serious talk is making me hungry. Plus I don't really watch my girlish figure much these days." Delia cackled delightfully and straightened the veil on her tiny black hat.

Gregory quickly prepared some appetizers and slid a beautifully arranged cheese place towards his former lover. As the old woman flashed a look towards the barkeep, Ada saw young Delia and young Gregory again.

"Carry on, my dear. You were getting to the best part."

"It is possible that one or both of you are an Arch Lumen, a head Luminary. Gregory believes Ada is one, which is why he wanted to speed up our little *lecture* earlier." Mathias gave the bartender the side eye before continuing.

"However, I'd say at this point in both of your development that it is hard to confirm each of your talents and roles in Ahm's army. What I *can* confirm is that you are Dyads, or two Luminaries who are attracted to each other like magnets, but not in a sexual way. In the human world, folklore has many Dyads pegged as twin flames. These people that just seem to constantly be drawn to one another. An Arch Lumen always has a super talented Lumen at their side that they aren't completely interested in as far as sex goes. You may have met couples who are always together but not in a sexual sense. They seem to finish each other's sentences, etcetera."

Ada let Mathias' words wash over her. At this point she was almost certain they didn't totally fit the mold for a Serf or a simple Dyad pair. She felt they were inexplicably drawn to each other in a non-sexual sense, but she didn't think either of them were ready to commit to each other as Dyads. She didn't think she was Arch Lumen material, though. *Maybe Chris.*

Ada shared her thoughts with Chris telepathically.

His thoughts entered her mind like soft waves. *I'm no Arch Lumen. And you're like a sister to me, but I'm not sure we're Dyads either.* Ada broke their silence, "Mathias, I'm not sure what I can commit to at this point. I don't match anything that you've described. At least not yet. Although new things keep happening every day. I guess I'd call it a progression."

A slow smile spread across Delia's wise face. As she began to speak, Ada noticed the room was filled with a heavy silence.

"Well my dear, I do have an example of a very surprising Dyad pair. This was well before your time. In the 1970's the governor of California was Elton Tisdale. He was the quintessential middle-aged, polished governor. He was married to Elaine Tisdale, a very beautiful socialite with ties to many wealthy families. Old money, as you'd say. Rumors got out that Governor Tisdale had an affair with a long time childhood friend, Susan. It turned out rumors were kicked off by the governor's secretary, who sold the story to the newspapers. It was alleged that Susan was always with the governor, everywhere he went, always at his office and finished his sentences. She'd worked on his campaign for governor and his campaign for president. Well, the governor himself was ugly as sin. But very charismatic. They were both hard on the eyes as you'd say. Much as we'd expect a Dyad pair to be, on the plain side visually. But still Luminaries. In fact they were well known among the Luminary community. The whole scandal cost governor Tisdale the presidency."

Mathias sat for a moment absorbing the story before finally saying, "I see your point, Delia. Arch Lumen are almost always visually appealing. I do remember governor Tisdale. He had a face like a potato. Please pardon bad the pun." Mathias sipped his drink.

Ada twisted her napkin in her lap, confused and nervous. She'd expected that they would find answers today, but not answers that created more confusion. She looked down at her rumpled napkin, then looked straight into Mathias' eyes. Questions swirled through her mind, and no one could misread the challenge in her eyes and voice as she began to speak.

"Your explanations provide clarity since some of it does match what both Chris and I have experienced, but you also raise many more questions. For example, I can initiate and control time by slowing it down or stopping it. I also have prophetic dreams. And I think I may have had a conversation with a seagull last week, like a *full-on* conversation in my head. *With a bird.* At the time I thought I was losing my marbles."

Gregory refilled her Chardonnay. Ada noticed as he disconcertedly ran his hands through his hair, it now stood wildly up on his head and he made no effort to tame it. He scurried about behind the bar tinkering. Delia had pulled an impossibly long cigarette out of her purse, and Gregory lit it for her. The old lady looked as aloof as a preening housecat. Ada took a long sip of the chilled wine and continued to question Mathias.

"I only just met Chris. While I like him, I certainly can't claim to be a Dyad tied to Chris, yet. Nor can I claim to be an Arch Lumen. I mean, don't get me wrong. I enjoy Chris and I would miss him in my life, but we just met a few days ago. Chris, what do you think?"

Ada had decided to verbalize her question to Chris, even

though she felt his thoughts permeating her mind, and he had the same feelings she did.

"I feel exactly the same way. This does answer quite a few questions, and that's a blessing. Obviously, I've never been like everyone else. I wasn't a normal kid. Neither was Ada, for that matter. We both knew that. We both knew weren't crazy. We've both had relatives that were as unusual or more so than we were."

Ada interjected more sheepishly this time. She couldn't afford to have Mathias view her in a bad light, and she really did like him. She needed him in her life just as much as she needed Chris. She needed to know what he knew. She needed his guidance.

"So how do we figure this out? What happens next?"

"I can provide more clarity. We will get answers over time for all of your questions. But I have to warn you, even I don't have all the answers. We don't have a *Luminary Encyclopedia* the to consult."

Delia began laughing with Mathias' last comment, and even tense Gregory began to chuckle. Mathias continued after cracking a smile and having a long sip of his drink.

"This is still trial and error for me, even after five hundred years. Every Luminary is different, and Arch Lumens, in particular, are very complicated creatures. Every reincarnation is different as well. The same soul that is passed on from body to body is a little different each time. This will be dangerous. You both need to take this very seriously, especially while we are trying to sort this all out. Luminaries are at their most vulnerable when they are children and when their powers begin to unfold and develop, making it difficult to control them."

Ada sat completely still, her entire body tense. She was absorbing all of the information, but it was quite overwhelming. Mathias continued on.

"The term *Luminary* serves more than one purpose for

those who are like you. When an ordinary person is infected by the Overlord, certain Luminaries are able to drain the dark energy out of the infected. It will appear as a ball of light that you can pull out and discard, which is why you are called a Luminary. I have seen it. The last time I saw it, it was in a redheaded reincarnation and descendent of Mary Magdalene."

Ada's jaw dropped open. Gregory looked even more anxious, if that was possible. Meanwhile, Delia sat as cool as a cucumber. Mathias continued on, matter-of-factly schooling his fresh-faced Luminaries as if he were teaching a history class to freshman at the University.

"I'm not entirely certain how these talents are passed down, but I did trace past versions of Ada back as far as Mary Magdalene."

Now he spoke directly to Ada. "You almost always have some trace of red in your hair, although it changes color in the light."

Mathias got up and was pacing around the bar with his drink as he talked.

Lectured. It's like a supernatural lecture.

He stopped and looked at his students to find them dumbfounded and staring at him a little shell shocked.

"The saints thing, now that is an interesting story. Saints with superpowers. We won't dig into that today though. Save that for another day, or maybe homework."

He then started laughing at his own joke. "Lumen homework. That's pretty funny."

No one else was laughing. Not even Delia.

"Finally, I truly do not like it when you bubble up and appear. None of us do. Here's why. It's always an imminent sign of something serious. All of the people like us, the Serfs, and the children I raised who are now adults, will work tirelessly and selflessly to help you. They self-sacrifice for the greater good when Mary appears and have been doing so for longer than I even know. This means many of them will die. Children even. Your presence is not regarded kindly by many when you surface."

Ada felt goosebumps rise up on her arms and back down her spine.

"This is why the owner of the theatre called you Mary. This is also why he was a bit rude. We had a bit of a debate about whether or not you are indeed Mary, Ada. Mostly because your talents are appearing in a slow and disjointed way. This either means you aren't Mary or that your powers are super strong and thus hard to manage—at least in the beginning. There is also an outside chance you could be a halfling, a Luminary who is half human."

Mathias continued pacing and gesturing with his free hand. His voice was strong, portraying confidence and strength but fell short of arrogance.

So fatherly. Like a supernatural patriarch looking after us. Her body was rapt with attention. *That confidence says this is real. It's evidence of the five hundred years he's spent doing this. Teaching the Luminaries. It is real. All of it.*

Mathias looked from Ada to Chris.

"Chris, I think you may come from a long line of guardians, simply known as Sentinel Lumens. They protect Arch Lumen."

Mathias sat down for a moment, and Gregory placed a plate of crab dip and garlic Naan bread out for them to snack on.

Delia cleared her whisky-soaked throat and began speaking. "If I may interject. They don't look like halflings, Mathias. They are both physically perfect. Ada is a sexual distraction for anything with a pulse. As is Chris. They look like gods, or should I say demi-gods. Look at Chris's musculature. He's obviously a Sentinel. Halflings are attractive from time to time, but they've never looked like these two. Nor do they have the abilities Ada mentioned. They typically have a few simple talents. But they don't look like Dyads to me either. Dyads are rarely beautiful on the outside. I mean, come on, we all know the running joke about Dyads is that they are only *pretty on the inside*. They are most certainly not as heavily muscled as Chris."

Gregory's anxiousness seemed to have dissipated miraculously after several drinks. He interjected his thoughts on the subject. "I am going to have to say I agree with Delia. Although to Mathias' point, I have seen some very talented and very attractive Luminaries from time to time. Not Arch Lumens, but garden variety Luminaries. However, Chris and Ada's talents don't point to simple Luminary." He gestured toward Chris and Ada.

Mathias clinked the ice around in his glass. The group sat silently for a few moments before Mathias began to speak again.

"When an Arch Lumen and Sentinel appear, Ahm reveals them with intention. There will be an event that shows us exactly what Chris and Ada are. I might add, it will be up to us to help them develop their potential, no matter what they are."

Chris shifted in his seat after taking a bite of the crab dip and Naan bread. The delicious scent of crab blended with garlic and cheese wafted through the air. He took a sip of his drink, appearing to gather his courage. "You know, it's all making sense now. So visiting the Boho Luna and everything that happened afterwards was supposed to happen? Somehow Ada's dream directed us to Mathias and Delia. It was the long way around for sure, but it was also the only way to help show us what was going on, I suppose. It seemed like it was hard for us, and we had to really focus on small details to get the answers we needed."

Mathias cleared his throat and began to clarify Chris'

understandable question. "Ahm sometimes appears to speak to us. It's not always clear, but Ahm is still speaking, even if it doesn't seem to make sense at the time. Transparency is not always part of how it works with Luminaries, and that is why you are a Luminary. You are blessed with the ability to seek and find answers where it appears there are none. You can shed light on what is happening. Remember even at your darkest hour, that you are still a Luminary, and there's a reason for that."

Ada was immersed in Mathias' explanation. She listened wide-eyed as the pieces fell together.

"The way you and Ada solved this riddle is how you will be able to help people in the future while you each hone your craft. You both have plenty to learn and plenty of work to do. All in due time. Much of this will happen on its own. Remember I am not just a Luminary, but a leader and a teacher for those typically more simple in terms of talents than you two are. Also understand there is much I don't know about you or what you can do. Over the last five hundred years I've seen quite a few Luminaries like Ada, but they were all slightly different in both appearance and talent."

"So what's next? We finish school and just continue the status quo?" *This answers so many questions but raises so many more. What is going to happen next?* She didn't realize she had been compulsively caressing the neck of the tequila bottle. Gregory carefully took it from her hands and poured her a double shot.

"Well Ada, one thing is for certain, I sure wouldn't call it status quo. It's going to be a wild ride, so buckle up. Especially if you are the Arch Lumen. Remember, you appear to us with your talents in a particular location for a reason . . . He paused to gather his thoughts. "Most immediately, you will finish school. Then you will go out into the workforce to pursue and subdue people working for the Overlord. Your job will entail varying degrees of closeness to your mark, maybe an uncomfortable proximity to people who I would describe as horrid at their best. Ahm will place a person in your path that is involved in something nefarious. It's up to you to identify the person and his or her associates. You must prevent them from hurting and infecting other people."

"Gregory, you dirty old goat." Delia's eyes settled on the decanter, and she seemed to see it with new eyes as she eyed Gregory suspiciously. "She's done with that particular bottle of tequila. I can't believe you still have it after all these years." There was a slightly hysterical edge to her voice along with anger.

Gregory didn't take the bait to argue with the old woman. "Take it easy. How about a shot of tequila from the special bottle for old times' sake, Delia? Hm? I've got a-uh-lovely sack of beets in the back to show you. Wasn't it a sack of beets we had a romp on last time? Wow, I've never seen a young lady so interested in the hue of my beets."

"Just put it away, you dirty Irish pig. But pour me another whiskey."

"Delia, it's ok. It's just tequila, I'll be fine." Ada looked into Delia's eyes and grabbed her arm, smiling.

"Oh boy girl, you'll be feeling fine all right."

She tutted through her teeth and shook her head while she watched the bartender disappear with the decanter of tequila.

Just as Delia had alluded, Ada started to feel the tequila truly take hold in earnest. Her cheeks began to flush and a hint of perspiration emerged on her brow. Her vision blurred and a remarkably pleasant buzz set in. "Chris can take me home. I'll be ok. Don't worry."

"I'll take you home, young lady. We're going to the same place. I have some lovely tea at home that will help you combat that special tequila." Delia patted Ada on her head as if she was a small confused child.

She was indeed quite inebriated and in no mood to argue with this particular small but feisty elderly woman. *Plus I wore a tea length dress just to make this aged but venerable old woman happy.*

Chapter Thirteen: Revelations

Ada woke to her cell phone buzzing on the dresser and warm sunlight streaming through the window. Her cat purred contentedly and appeared angry as she gently hoisted him to the end of the bed to scramble out of bed for the phone. It was Chris. She groggily answered.

"Morning, sunshine!"

"What time is it. I feel like I just went to bed."

"It's the crack of ten. You slept until 10. I bet your cat is furious. Want me to come over and read his mind? See what he really thinks of you?"

"Whoa, whoa, whoa there, Mr. Sunshine. You must be a morning person. Let me get a cup of coffee down. How about brunch at Lilly's cafe down by the harbor."

"We have so much to talk about. I have some ideas."

"I have some, too. Right now they involve coffee and a shower. Meet you at 11?"

"Sounds good."

She brewed up a quick cup of coffee in a French press, fed the cat and hopped in the shower. She decided to go comfy on the outfit and paired a Unicorn T-shirt and yoga pants with a matching jacket. *How appropriate. I am indeed a unicorn. Who knew? And I thought I was just an angsty redhead.*

She did her best to comb through her wild tangles of hair before giving up and throwing it in a messy bun on top of her head. She grabbed her laptop and a notebook before slipping out her door. She walked gingerly down the stairs and peered around the corner at Delia's apartment. No sign of her. No weird flower smells. No cold air. She walked out into the crisp fall air and warm sunshine. She inhaled the wonderful smells of fall and drove away. Soft jazz played in the car as she made her way to the harbor café. She made a mental note to avoid the seagull.

Ada scanned the room in search of Chris' hulking frame. He was sitting in the back of the café attempting to be inconspicuous, but enormous men who looked like models did not blend in with everyone else. Chris had already ordered two pumpkin spice coffees and two enormous cinnamon rolls. The coffee was served in oversized mugs and topped with copious amounts of whip cream. The rolls had giant dollops of cream cheese icing dripping down them.

Delicious scents of fall drifted up to Ada's nose, making her stomach grumble. "OMG. You must've read my mind. Those look so delicious."

He cut his in half with a butter knife and licked the icing off the blade gingerly. "Mmm . . . *orgasmic*. You've got to try yours. That pumpkin spice coffee is divine. We are in for a treat."

"After what happened last night, I feel like I could chase this roll with a pizza. You know, some good old-fashioned stress binging. Geeesh. By the way, if Delia ever offers you tea, hard pass."

Ada wrapped her hands around her throat and pretended to choke to death.

"No matter how old and cute she looks, no tea. It tasted like total ass. If you could make a tea out of ass stank."

"Are you sure it was tea? I mean after yesterday, I suspect it was magical potion. A witch's brew."

Ada shook her head and sipped her coffee, the wheels turning in her mind. A long slow grin spread across her face. "Did you watch any of the *Elvish in Fairyland* movies when you were a kid?"

"Of course. I had all the action figures and a troll wand. My sister got a cauldron one birthday complete with the Elvish potions book and play potions. Every time I turned around she was stirring that pot and trying to get us all to drink her concoctions." Chris pretended to stir pretend cauldron with his coffee spoon.

"So where's our potions book? Or spell book? Something like that?"

"Yeah. Why didn't they offer us a book?"

"Maybe they don't know if we should know their secrets yet? Think about it. I live with my mind and my life, and I know it's super bizarre and I'm having a hard time believing what they said. It's all so shocking. Like maybe we aren't worth trusting just yet."

Chris stared out into the distance. He appeared to be gathering himself before telling her something. She'd never seen him quite so apprehensive. "Shocking is an understatement. I don't know about you but things just keep getting weirder by the day for me. Last night after the Boho something happened on my way home. I saw a cat get hit by a car. Right in front of me. So I stopped and got out. Its legs were most definitely broken and there was blood everywhere.

I kneeled down beside it and put my hands on its tiny broken body and felt this strange humming pulse inside my hands. Its eyes opened up. Then it began purring and darted away as if its legs weren't broken just a minute ago."

"I would feign surprise and say something expected like, *no way*, except I am not surprised. Unfortunately."

They sat in silence eating and sipping coffee. Ada enjoyed Chris' presence but was not ready to talk about the future. She could feel that he felt the same way. The air was heavy with their combined anxiety about what was to come next.

She took the last bite of her cinnamon roll. "So Mathias is the man with answers."

"He is, but he seemed to have them but not have them."

Ada stirred her coffee and tapped the spoon on the cup. She felt more curious at this point than concerned. *So many questions.* She pondered the lack of answers for a moment more before she decided she wanted to hear what Chris thought.

"So the question isn't just *what didn't he tell us.* There's also *why didn't he tell us.*"

Chris frowned as the door she'd opened allowed a flood of new concerns washed over him. "Can we trust him? Should we? What was in that old bat's tea?"

Ada reached across the table and grabbed his hand. "Chris. Breathe. Deep down, I think we should trust all three of them."

"You're right, Ada. I can be overly cautious and protective."

Ada smiled, closing her eyes for a moment to gather her thoughts. *There is a bright side.* "You know what, Chris? Today is better than yesterday because we have each other. Now, we have Mathias, Delia, and Gregory, too. They did create more questions and more anxiety. But at least we won't navigate that alone."

"So what's next?"

Ada shrugged her shoulders but remembered Mathias' words the night before. "They said things would just happen."

"Are you comfortable just waiting to see what fresh hell awaits us next?"

"No way. We will be totally off guard just like all the other times."

The waitress came over just then, a frumpy middle-aged woman with a crown of graying hair piled up in a bun she didn't bother to color. She was cheerful and oblivious to the weighty air hanging around their conversation.

"Another pumpkin spice coffee? Or just a regular top off of plain Joe?" Her smile lit up her plump cheeks. Her eyes narrowed at the end of the smile. "Sometimes simple is better."

Ada held her cup out for a top off and Chris slid his towards the coffee pot reluctantly.

As her plump bottom sashayed away, Ada noticed a tattoo on the back of her neck. It was a faded eye with three bars below it, partially obscured by a stray puff of gray hair. "Hmm. Didn't take her for the tattoo type."

Chris stole a quick glance and wrinkled his eyebrows. "Didn't take her for the *neck* tattoo type. I mean, come on, ladies don't usually do neck tattoos."

Ada lowered her voice to a whisper.

"That's so weird. Plain coffee? So not better than pumpkin spice. What kind of person is she?"

Chris leaned in and started to smile. He winked at Ada cheekily. "Yep, it's not the granny bun and the neck tattoo that's weird. All about that plain Jane Joe instead of the pumpkin spice crack."

Ada rolled her eyes and sipped her coffee.

"Some things are better simple. Coffee is not one of those things." A lightbulb went off at that moment for Ada. She sat up in her seat and held up one finger. "I know what to do. Which of our most recent events was the most softball?"

"That's easy. The Vogue ghost. The ghost at the Boho felt like it was trying to kill us with exploding glass. I think we will save that one for when we are smarter."

"I agree. Let's do some more research on the ghost. Want to hit the library?"

"It's as good a place as any to start."

"What show is at the Vogue now?"

"Not sure. We can look that up to. Maybe we should go sometime during a show to see if the extra energy feeds the ghost. I read that somewhere. Not sure if it's true or not."

"Great idea. Maybe we try and find some info on ghosts as well."

Half an hour later they were hard at work at the library microfiche machine scanning articles. They searched for a while before she finally found something. "So I searched for Garrett, the baron's assistant. But there were too many people with the name Garrett, so I looked under *Garrett* and *railroad*, and hit jackpot. Look at this."

Chris leaned over and read the article title from her screen.

"*Railroad Baron's Worker, Garrett Phar, Sentenced to Life in Prison for Rape and Murder of a Teenaged Syilx Okanagan Nation Girl.*"

Chris's mouth fell open, then he continued reading the rest of the article. "*Nahun Wenox, aged 15, was found beaten, raped, and bound in the cellar of Garrett Phar's home. Her father went to check on her after she did not return from working at Phar's home one evening. Nahun was found alive and taken to the hospital where she released a statement via translator. She alleged Garrett raped her and cut off her breast as punishment for not agreeing to consensual sex. Her father mentioned that Nahun is not the first girl from the Okanagan Nation to go missing after working for Phar. The police have been unsuccessful in locating any bodies on Phar's property. The railroad baron had no comments on the matter and did not attend Phar's sentencing. Rumor has it the baron had his suspicions regarding Garrett's nefarious activities and hired Phar to be his henchman.*"

Dread filled the pit of her stomach. "Chris, he's a pretty awful person. He could be the killer. When I was at the theatre in the dressing room, I received an image of Imogene nursing baby Eugene in the dressing room, like it was one of her last memories. Do you think he killed her while she was nursing the baby?"

Chris shook his head, clearly disgusted by the idea. "Oh man, I don't even want to think about it. It's so revolting. He sounds pretty hideous. He cut off that girl's breast, so he could kill a woman feeding a baby. I wonder if there's a way to figure anything else out with the prophetic dreams you have. Let's get some books on seeing the future and ghosts. I mean, some of it is going to be complete garbage, but maybe some of it has a grain of truth."

She printed off the article and analyzed the picture of Garrett that accompanied the text. He was short but stocky, the proverbial fire plug. His hands were beefy, his jaw thick and square. His eyes were small and piggish, devoid of emotion. They were like looking into bottomless pools of emptiness. Just like Mathias said, his expression was like looking into an abyss.

"Ada, I'm sure some of it will be total nonsense. But it's possible something useful will come up. We really don't have any other choice. I mean, since there is no encyclopedia of luminary."

They stopped by the paranormal section and grabbed several books. As they were checking out, the librarian reached behind the counter and shuffled a few books around. Finally she emerged from below the counter with a velvet-bound book in hand.

"If you are researching the paranormal, I highly recommend this particular book."

She appeared to be in her early thirties with the beginning of crow's feet at the corner of her eyes. Her skin was a super pale cream that matched her equally pale hair, which was the color of sun-bleached sand. Her hair was cropped tight to her head and her eyes were a strange pale hazel. When Ada looked into her eyes, she had a strange De Ja Vu moment that she couldn't explain. *Is she one of us?* Unsure of how to proceed, she simply thanked her and added the book to her stash.

It was too much for her to read on her own, so they decided to divide and conquer. Chris agreed to text her that evening if he came across anything useful. Armed with the print-out and some library books, they set out to put a century old murder to rest.

CHAPTER FOURTEEN: CHANGES

Cuddled up in her PJ's on the couch, Ada began the arduous task of rooting through the stack of books. *What am I even looking for? A needle in a haystack, that's what.* The first book took her over an hour and then she decided it was essentially garbage. It seemed contrived, and nothing seemed real to her or helpful. The second book was much of the same.

She decided to take a break and prepared a cup of strong coffee in her French press, then spiked it with a little dark rum. Eying the bottle of rum, she grabbed a shot glass out of the cabinet. It was blue with a gold leaf image of the city of Cincinnati on the front. There was a chip on the lip from one of her parents' many moves. She had always been fond of this tiny glas,s and memories of her mother flooded back to her as she turned it over in her hands. She poured herself a shot of straight rum and tossed it back. She grimaced. The alcohol burned its way down her throat as she poured another shot. If nothing else, she was going to let her hair down while she read through this nonsensical made-up supernatural garbage. *If I of all people think it's garbage, it is straight bullshit.*

After the third shot, she had the radio turned up and started dancing around her apartment. She picked up a candlestick and began to sing along to the radio. She jumped up on the couch and pretended it was a stage. Mr. Jiggles sat in front of the TV eyeing her suspiciously. He was clearly not enjoying her off key serenade. A head banging tune came on and she flipped her wild hair around with total abandon. Finally, a giggle rose to the surface and she felt her worries slip away.

She collapsed on the couch in a pile of wild hair and tangled long legs. She took a deep breath and suddenly felt the candlestick warm in her hands. Jumping up she eyed it suspiciously. She'd been dancing around with Delia's fancy candlestick—but she'd returned those to her. Then she looked over at the counter and noticed a note and a strange-looking candle. It had flowers and leaves suspended in the wax. She hopped up and examined the candle. It smelled faintly of lilac. The post-it note said absolutely nothing, just *XO, Delia*. She decided to light the candle on the weird candlestick. *Why the fuck not? Maybe it will help.*

She grabbed her coffee off the counter and sat back down on the couch. The third book was titled simply *The Undead* and had an image of an eye with three bars below it. *Wait a minute . . . .That's the old ladies tattoo from the café.* She ran her hands over the unique cover, studying it cautiously. *Not a coincidence.* No author listed. No publisher. No introduction, and no synopsis. The cover was a smooth charcoal velvet, and the title was in raised metal. She sniffed the book, and the odors of incense and lavender wafted up. The pages were a yellowed waxy paper. The pages appeared to be handwritten in an old-fashioned prose with pen and ink. Mr. Jiggles cuddled back up with her, satisfied that her off key serenade was over and things were back to status quo.

After a few chapters she texted Chris and let him know that she thought she'd hit the jackpot. Many aspects of the text appeared like the others—nothing more than made-up conjecture. But some of it seemed correct and resonated with her on a fundamental level, specifically the chapters on prophetic dreams and ways to reach the undead. It mentioned immersing yourself in the location of the haunting to better reach the undead. She read that in some cases, touching the items they held dear could unleash a replay of an event or strong feelings. With prophetic dreams, it mentioned focusing on the location in question or an item associated with the issue prior to bedtime. Puzzled, Ada realized she'd always focused prior to bedtime in order to get a release of information in her dreams.

She texted Chris, and they decided that tomorrow they needed to pop into the Vogue in the morning before class to see if Michael might allow them to sleep over. As much as it creeped them both out, they decided it had to be done. Ada drifted off to sleep on the couch with the book still in her hands.

She awoke the next morning after a night devoid of dreams. She looked at the candle on the counter, suspicious about whether it was used to block the spirits or open her mind to them. It seemed more like the latter. She hopped up and brewed some coffee before hitting the shower. She dressed in some comfy sweats and a simple tank top. A quick detangle of her hair and a little lip gloss, and she was ready for the day. She grabbed her backpack tossed the Undead book in along with her laptop, then grabbed an old sleeping bag she used to use for camping. She poured the coffee into two thermoses, one for her and for Chris. She bounded down the hall and down the stairs, out into the crisp fall air.

She met Chris in the vestibule at the Vogue. He greeted her with a big dreamy model smile, and a plain white T shirt hugged his beefy toned body. *Why do I feel absolutely no attraction to him?* It was odd, because he was hot by any woman's measuring stick.

"Let's do this." She crossed her fingers in the air for luck in front of Chris before awkwardly opening the vestibule door with her cumbersome backpack and entering the main entry. Michael peered out at them from the ticket counter, his eyes partially obscured by a set of neon pink readers adorned with bling on both sides. He did not look remotely surprised. It was like he knew they were coming. *Why would he be sitting behind the ticket counter this early in the morning?*

"Mary. So nice to see you." He hopped up and came around the counter. "What can I do for you?"

She eyed him somewhat suspiciously. He'd called her Mary again, which was off putting, and he just seemed a little strange or off in general to her. *Must be halflings have gifts like second sight?*

Michael clasped his hands together in front him and rubbed them together, smiling wolfishly. There seemed to be copious amounts of gleaming white teeth flashing at her, as if he were ready to consume kittens. Unperturbed, she moved forward with their plan.

"We thought maybe we could check out the dressing room again this morning. Just for a few moments?"

"Sure. We've continued to have issues back there, and great granny seems to be more wound up than ever. One of my best actors has been dressing in the hall. It's so degrading. I'm just waiting for him to quit." He drug out the word waiting dramatically, and loudly.

Oh good. He's still pissed about the haunting. I bet he cooperates.

Chris cleared his throat, his gaze settling on Ada with an uncharacteristic stony seriousness. He elbowed her lightly. "Also, Michael, we thought we would spend the night. Tonight. I picked up this book at the library. It was a suggestion in the book."

"By all means. Anyone crazy enough to spend the night back there can have at it. Not even I would sleep over back there. And its my great granny at work. Go right on ahead." He waved them on towards the back of the theatre.

Ada did as she was told, stealing a peek back at Michael as they walked away. He was all but salivating over Chris' taut and firm backside. Making no effort to hide his feelings, he made a *mmm, mmm* sound, like someone enjoying a scrumptious puffed pastry.

As they made their way around to the back of the theatre where the dressing rooms were, it again grew cold. Slowly the smell of cigars wafted through as well. No sounds of crying were heard this time, though.

They stopped at the threshold of Imogene's doorway, and Ada took a deep, head-clearing breath to gather some courage. "So, Chris, the book said to touch any items that may have been present in the room when the ghost was alive. If the original floors are present, it also suggested removing shoes and walking barefoot in the room. What did you read?"

Chris confirmed her findings. "One I read mentioned the same thing, touching time period items that the spirit would have had living contact with. But it didn't say anything about shoe removal. So oddly specific . . . Can't hurt to try, though."

As soon as Ada cleared the threshold of the doorway, she smelled the faint scent of flowers from an old-fashioned perfume. She walked around the room while Chris stood protectively watching near the doorway. She ran her hands over the mirror in the corner and over the dressing table. There was an antique velvet-covered chaise in the corner, and she sat down. Against her better judgement, she decided to lie down and closed her eyes. She felt the weight of her hair as it spilled over the side.

"Ada, are you sure about that? Could that be the place where she was actually murdered?" His tone echoed the concern he felt as his protective instincts kicked in.

"Why not? Walk around, Chris, touch a few things. It can't hurt for us both to try."

He made a mediocre effort at touching items and sat down in the threshold of the doorway.

Ada looked over at him with her brows furrowed. "Close your eyes, Chris. Let's give this a real try."

He did as told, and she closed hers again as well. The minutes ticked by, and soon Ada began to daydream.

A heavily muscled man lay on top of her, his erect and sizeable cock pressing uncomfortably against her vagina through layers and layers of expensive silk fabrics. Ada opened her eyes in her dream to see the cold face of Garrett. His rough hands pulled at the bodice of her dress until her breasts were exposed. She heard his gravely voice begin to speak as he rubbed his rough unshaven face against her neck, hungrily kissing her with savage abandon.

"I heard you are entertaining gentleman callers, Imogene. Is that true?"

"As long as you don't mark up the merchandise, Garrett. My fee to entertain the likes of you is three hundred dollars. I have another caller visiting after you. You have until half past noon to finish."

"Oh, I heard all about your other caller. I bet you won't need the baron's big cock after I get done with you, you dirty little tramp."

"As I said Garrett, don't mark up the merchandise. No kissing. No ass sex."

"Oh. I can be quick."

He sat up and began pawing hungrily through the layers of her expensive gown. Finally he made it through and slid his mouth hungrily over her vagina, slipping his tongue inside to make her ready for his rock-hard cock.

She grabbed the back of his head and moaned.

"I'm ready, baby. Make me scream. No one is here to hear it." He pulled out his cock, now dripping with semen. He was so wide she almost yelled out as he filled her completely with his first pump into her ample hips. She felt like he was fucking her like a wild animal, making no effort to make sure he wasn't hurting her. He fucked her so hard her head hit the dressing room wall, but he still didn't come.

Out of exasperation, she wriggled out from under him, hiked up her dresses and bent over the chaise.

"Come on, baby. Make it hurt."

Before she could stop him, he pushed his rock-hard cock into her ass. Her breath caught and before she could cry out, he pumped her until she came.

"How's that, you dirty bitch. No ass sex, hm? You like it though,

don't you."

With her breath still heaving in her chest, he grabbed her roughly and threw her back on the chaise lounge. He grabbed her breasts so hard tears welled up in her eyes. He grabbed her legs and wrapped them around his neck and entered her hot and wet vagina again.

"Take my cum, you nasty whore."

He squeezed her breast again and finished, taking pleasure in her pain. He pulled out his cock afterwards, zipped his pants up and threw the money across her half naked body. She jerked as the coins and bills struck her bare skin.

"I'll be back next week after payday. Before the baron. I'm not taking his sloppy seconds."

With that he stormed out of the room.

Ada woke up with a startled jump and sat up. Her underwear felt moist and her breasts actually felt tender. She rubbed them gingerly and looked around. Chris had fallen completely asleep sitting in the doorway with his head against the jam.

"Chris! What time is it? We'll be late for class."

Startled, he scrambled around to pull his phone out of his back pocket. "We've only been here fifteen minutes."

"What? No way. I just fell asleep and had a dream, the whole bit."

"Well, it's only been fifteen minutes. Wait, you said you had a dream?"

"Yeah. Imogene was turning tricks. Garrett was a client. So was the baron."

"That's not super surprising. It doesn't explain who killed her though, does it?"

"No, not so far. Garrett liked it rough, but he didn't try to kill her in my dream. This chaise lounge has seen some miles, though. I think it was here when Imogene used this room."

She wrinkled her nose and pulled her hand away from the stained velvet.

"Let's get to class," Chris responded. "We can meet here afterward and order pizza. Maybe you will get more overnight, like the book said." He tossed her some hand sanitizer from her backpack before they slipped quietly out of Imogene's dressing room. She noted that Chris' pace was brisk. He seemed to be keen on avoiding Michael and his roving eyes. If one could be sexually assaulted visually, Michael could pull it off. They slipped out a back door and rode to class together. She was eager to see Mathias again.

CHAPTER FIFTEEN: ONWARD

Class was uneventful. Mathias' voice was both soothing and painfully boring. After experiencing the bizarre incidents of the week, sitting through a lecture on fundamentals of alleged supernatural happenings was mundane.

Ada noted that Mathias did a very thorough job of shedding light on multiple theories. However, they were just that, theories. All were close to the truth that she and Chris were living, but not quite spot on. He quoted several authors who studied the paranormal with a scientific bent, those who had credibility in the world of science and were not considered garden variety kooks. She found her mind drifting from the lecture to the events of the past few days.

What is with Delia's candelabra and strange candles? Where did that weird handwritten book come from? She couldn't wait for class to end so they could read more of the strange book at the theatre over pizza. She resisted the urge to pull it out of her backpack during the lecture.

Mathias flipped the lights off and pulled down a large screen. He began the second part of the day's lecture, videos of unexplained paranormal events. There was a projector in the ceiling that was connected to his laptop. After a few minutes he had the videos started and all eyes were on the screen.

As her fellow students *mhmm-ed* and *hawed* in surprise, she herself was far from shocked. Giving in to her curiosity, she reached into her bag and pulled out the velvet covered book.

Chris leaned over and decided to quietly pull his desk over

to hers to get a better view.

Ada laid the book inside her notebook. They both pretended to take notes on the presentation.

She opened the book slowly to the first page only to find it completely blank. The next page was the same way. Disappointed and confused, she thumbed quickly through several more. The writing was completely gone. She shut it quickly and looked at the cover to make sure she'd grabbed the correct book. Shaking her head, she looked at Chris.

His beautifully perfect face reflecting furrowed brows back at her. He grabbed it and opened it, thumbed through a few pages only to reveal the same blank pages.

Just then, the lights flicked back on and students began hurriedly packing up as the class bell sounded.

Mathias' voice boomed over the chaos.

"Remember our off-site lesson for Thursday will be at Craigdarroch Castle. Much appreciation to Kevin and family for allowing us to enter the castle for the lecture."

Mathias appeared out of nowhere and ran his hands over the velvet cover and metal-inlayed title. He opened the book to reveal the blank pages and began laughing. He shut his eyes for a moment tapped his temple with an index finger deep in thought. He went to a cabinet in the back of the room and unlocked it after rifling around his pocket for the key. After rummaging around inside and knocking some things over, he emerged with a small tealight-sized candle that looked the same as the one Delia had left in Ada's apartment. He also had a small cup made of the same strange stone that the candelabra contained.

"Aha! I knew I had one." He brought the items over to Chris and Ada.

She turned the cold stone over in her hands. The shiny flecks of gold caught the light the same way Delia's candlestick did.

Chris picked up the tea light and smelled it cautiously.

"The Undead Text only reveals its secrets if you block dark souls from its vicinity with this specific candle. The candle is a special blend of flowers and herbs blessed by a high-order Luminary that is also a priest. Side note, sage is very good at blocking all spirits. Be careful with sage, because if you have any sage in the room with the Undead book, you may not get answers. The sage is too strong, and it simply knocks out everything."

As Mathias rambled on about sage, Ada was hung up on what he'd said just before that. It was strange he had so much to say about sage and was not expanding on Luminary priests. Bringing up the sage and acting like Luminary priests were a side car was like putting a bandaid on a compound fracture. She raised her right hand, palm forward, gesturing for Mathias to stop. Her eyes wrinkled closed in confusion. "Whoa, whoa, wait. Could we, uh, back up for a moment. There are priests that are Luminaries? Doesn't that kind of go against the teachings of organized religion today?"

Chris interjected as well, just as confused. "It conflicts with all organized religion. Not just one religion. *All religion.* There's not one religion I've studied that mentions anything that is going on with us, Ada."

Mathias paused a moment to collect his thoughts. "Contrary to popular belief, the Bible — as well as all other religious books from the last several thousand years — are in part true. However, they are not entirely true down to each and every letter. There are correct elements, but somewhere along the way things were not taken down correctly and the message was distorted, most likely because actual Luminaries are not allowed to write down anything on paper about what they know or what they do. It's too dangerous. They are also forbidden from fraternizing too closely with mortals. That's why there is no book or handbook for me to give you. The Undead

Book is an anomaly in that it only reveals its writing to Luminaries under specific circumstances. In other words, there can't be any negative energy in the room. Hence Delia's candles. The book also changes each time you open it. Think of it more as a tool to view or contact another world and less as a book."

"You mean sort of like a Ouija Board," she suggested, trying to understand Mathias.

"Sort of. If the Ouija board contained a hyper chip and was more than a piece of simple cardboard. The Undead Text is so complicated most of us can't ever get it to do anything. Myself included. I tried. About two hundred years ago. Clearly it must have worked for you two, or you wouldn't have looked so dejected when nothing happened when you opened it in class. And yes, I noticed you weren't paying attention to my lecture."

He laughed and smiled deviously at both of them before continuing.

"I hate to say this, but not all the students in the classroom are pure and good souls. In fact, I'd say there's a few that are downright rotten. But that's a story for another day."

"Meathhead," Ada and Chris both shouted.

"I'm sorry. Meathead? Who's this meathead you speak of?" Mathias asked.

Ada attempted to contain a giggle that bubbled up and she put her hand on Mathias's arm. "It's Kevin."

"Oh, yeah. That Kevin kid. Bad blood there. I don't mean that facetiously. He's the railroad baron's descendant. There's some local negative blood or bad DNA with that family for sure. Just like you are a descendant of Mary Magdalene, or so I believe, he's a descendant of something more sinister. I've been following that family for centuries. I'm not kidding. They are escalating with every new generation."

Chris shook his head in agreement. "It's like every day

more things makes sense for us. For both of us."

"Oh, I'll bet. As time passes more and more will come into focus for both of you. Well, I've got an appointment to get to. Be safe, you two. Baby steps. Don't bite off more than you can chew just yet."

After picking up pizza and beer, they drove to the Vogue Theatre. The air was crisp and overcast, heavy with pending rain and a possible storm. *How appropriate. Nice and scary.* They pulled up just in time for the rain to let loose. Cracks of thunder shattered the dark sky. They made a run for it, along with their sleeping bags, backpacks, beer, and pizza. The rain and thunder along with the mad dash was invigorating. They burst into the theatre laughing and full of life and energy.

Michael greeted them at the door. His eyes full with a mischievous twinkle. "There you are. Look at that storm." He crossed his arms in front of his body and tilted his head, still smiling. "So . . . How long do you think you'll make it?"

"Well Michael, we will be fine. We have planned ahead and have beer and pizza. What else do you need in a haunted theatre overnight?"

They all started laughing.

"Well kids, let me give you my cell and contact info in case anything too scary happens. I live close by and can be here at a moment's notice. I'll be back tomorrow morning at seven."

He handed Ada his business card and locked them in the theatre. The tumbling locks clicking together made her realize that this was real. It was happening. She was spending the night in a haunted theatre with a friend she'd just met a few weeks ago. She looked at Chris, feeling ever so slightly anxious.

He smiled reassuringly back at her. "Don't worry. What's the worst that could happen? Plus we have beer."

"You're so right, Chris. This is going to be fun. Let's go

poke around the stage and eat. I'm starving, and this pizza smells heavenly. No pun intended."

They sat on the stage under the lights eating and chatting. The beer was cold and took the edge off. This was the most carefree Ada had felt since she'd lost her parents. She really felt a connection with Chris.

Ada hopped up on the table that was sitting on the stage. "So who is this . . ." She arched her back and tossed her hair provocatively. "Oh meathead! You're so brainless and handsome." She twirled a long gingery lock around her finger.

"Oh, that's funny. I could never understand what girls saw in him. He's a total toad."

"I know what they see in him. A lifetime of designer handbags and mani-pedi's over mimosas. The NFL interest in him is like catnip for entitled rotten-to-the-core girls."

"It almost seems like it's more than that. You know? But I can't quite put my finger on it. Like some sort of strange magnetic pull."

"I know what you mean. And then there's what Mathias alluded to today about bloodlines or whatever it was. I'm still having a hard time buying all that Mary Magdalene hocus pocus."

"I know, Ada. I struggle to believe it, but then it all makes so much sense all at the same time."

"Someday maybe it will come together."

"One step at a time. Things are already making more sense for both of us. Don't you think?"

"Sort of. I guess." She shrugged and chugged a beer. She exhaled long and slow as she felt the beer kicking in. She turned her gaze to Chris. He was devouring the last of pizza, none too politely. "You ready?"

He gobbled the last bit down and washed it down with beer. Holding one finger up as he swallowed hastily before answering. "Yep. It's dark outside, it's storming, and we are a little drunk."

"So what you're saying is it's the perfect time for a ghostly sleepover." She smiled, expressing more confidence than she actually felt.

They headed back to Imogene's dressing room a little reluctantly. It was feeling more real now that they had to actually go into the room. A boom of thunder shook the theatre as lightning struck close by. Ada screamed and grabbed Chris. A chunk of plaster fell from the ceiling and the lights went out.

Chris screamed, too.

A minute of silence in the darkness passed before they both started laughing. Chris took a deep breath and turned on his cellphone flashlight.

They crept down the stairs and down the hallway. The cloying smell of mildew was slowly overtaken by the odor of cigar smoke. The faint smell of perfume grew stronger as they got closer to Imogene's room. No weeping this time. They stopped at the doorway to her dressing room.

Chris' strong baritone broke the silence. "Should we get out the candle?"

"No, Mathias said it would block the bad energy. I think we need to see what the bad energy has to present. Besides, these don't seem to be as crazy bad. Compared to the ones at the Boho, at least."

"Since we now know Garrett to be a homicidal rapist and murderer? Do you still think Boho is softball?"

"You're so right, Chris. I think we thought we were taking the easy one and we took the worst one. But we should save that candle for when we really need it. Like if something happens like the exploding glass at Boho. If Garrett is here, which he might not be, we need to know what he has to say. If we get the candle out, we have no opportunity to see what he, the baron, or anyone with bad energy might have to say."

"Ok. But at the first sign of any crazy train shit, the candle is getting lit." He settled his gaze on her just a second too long.

It was a warning to be careful, and she took heed. She watched as he set up his sleeping bag next to the chaise lounge. She decided to try the chaise again, no matter how gross. She unrolled her sleeping bag by the light of Chris' cellphone. She looked around the room, wondering if there might be a normal candle somewhere. She saw a large cinnamon scented pillar on one of the dressing tables.

"Perfect, that way my cellphone won't die." She rifled around her bag, pulled out some matches, and lit the candle. After kicking off her shoes, she settled into her sleeping bag on the chaise lounge. She reached down and grabbed Chris' hand. Feeling reassured by his presence, Ada decided to move forward and attempt to contact Imogene again in a dream state to see what else she could share.

"Here goes."

"I'm right here with you. Nothing to worry about."

She closed her eyes and let the thoughts from the day pass through her mind. She began to focus on Imogene. Sure enough, just as the book said, the dream came.

Looking down, she could see she was wearing a beautiful period gown in red silk and black lace. Her dainty gloved hand held an ice-cold crystal flute of champagne. She walked down a marble-floored corridor and could see a set of enormous doors at the end of the hall that were open. People dressed extravagantly were dancing in a grandly sized ballroom. As she walked into the ballroom, she felt all eyes on her. Hushed whispers circulated around the room.

Suddenly feelings of jealousy from the women around the room permeated her mind as the stares began to feel more like stabbing knives. Lustful thoughts bombarded her from varying directions around the room.

At that moment Ada realized she was aware of her dream state and maintained some sense of her own consciousness. She wasn't just a passenger in the dream or watching a movie reel. It then dawned on her that Imogene must have been a Luminary. She felt other people's feelings, too.

Imogene made her way to a corner table in the back, free of roving eyes, and gingerly sat the champagne flute down. She still felt a powerful gaze watching her from afar. Feelings of carnal lust and darkness came through. She felt a magnetic pull towards him despite the fact that she knew he had a dark side. Glancing up, she instantly locked gazes with the railroad baron. He sat at a large table at the head of the room. His blonde-haired and blue-eyed wife, Vivian, was at his side. She was dressed in a stunning pale-blue silk gown that matched her cold eyes perfectly. Stunning topaz jewels adorned her delicate ears and thin neck. She looked around the room, unabashedly making no effort to hide her boredom. Vivian's eyes caught Garrett's. He was seated near the baron's table but not at it.

From her vantage point, Imogene could see Garrett shift in his seat and smile smugly at Vivian as he took a sip of his high ball. She blushed and looked away, appearing preoccupied with some food on her plate. Ada watched through Imogene's eyes as Garrett excused himself from his table, with Vivian following none too discretely a few moments later. Curiosity got the best of her and she slipped back out of the ballroom using the same side hall they had.

She heard giggles and footsteps, and she followed quietly with cat-like grace. She peered around the corner in time to see the edges of a pale blue silk dress disappear into the servant quarters before a heavy oak door slammed and locks tumbled. She knew which servant's room that was, as she'd visited it herself a time or two, although there wasn't much giggling when Garrett ravaged her body. She tiptoed the rest of the way down the hall and pressed her ear up against door. She heard the unmistakable sound of a woman in the throes of sexual agony. Garrett was pounding her so hard it sounded like the bed might give way. Better her than me, Imogene thought. Such a vile man. Hitching up her skirts, she hurried away. Her ample breasts jiggling provocatively down the hall.

Once she rounded the corner, there stood the baron with one hand on his hip. Drink in hand, he smiled at her. He looked down at the marble floor and shook his head. He knows about Vivian and Garret, *Imogene realized. As she grew closer, she felt his feelings, an emptiness in his heart. A coldness along with simmering anger. Eager to distract him, she slipped her body up next to his as she was passing him. Just a little too close. She brushed her breast against his arm and blew him a kiss as she passed by. Her perfume wafted around him in an intoxicating cloud. She felt his anger dissipate to be replaced by lust. His eyes locked with hers and she felt them on her back as she walked back to the party. She wiggled her bottom and took her time walking back, swinging her hips with every step.*

The noise and activity of the ballroom was a welcome change from the tenseness of the baron's mood. She made her way back to her table in the back and sat down. A crème brulee sat waiting for her along with fresh coffee, spiked with her favorite imported Caribbean rum. She took her time and enjoyed people watching from her vantage point at the back of the room. Soon a servant brought her another coffee. As she lifted the cup, she found a small handwritten note on the saucer. It said simply the red room.

She finished her second coffee and left the ballroom again unnoticed. She knew her way to the red room and took a back stairway in the servant's section of the mansion to make sure no one saw her. There were a number of men in the ballroom who were current or past clients. Sneaking off down a well traversed hallway unaccompanied in the castle would spur gossip and rumors.

She made her way up the winding narrow stairway to the fourth floor. The red room was an ornate corner suite normally used for visiting dignitaries. She knew no one entered the fourth floor much and it was a very discreet location for their trysts. I wonder where Baron and Vivian sleep. Do they sleep together? *Imogene* mused.

The key for the suite was under a vase in a small stone grotto at the end of the hall. She passed by painting after painting of the baron's deceased family members. She always thought they were looking down on her as she walked by. She shivered and grabbed the key quickly. Tucking it into the sleeve of her dress, she then hurried back towards the suite. She unlocked the door and slipped into the room undetected. She closed the door behind her and locked it. Leaning her back against the wall she exhaled. Trying not to get caught fucking the richest man in Vancouver was both exhilarating and terrifying at the same time.

There was a long hallway before the suite's sitting room. It was lined on both sides with bookshelves and artwork. She ran her hands over the gilded tomes, some bound in leather some not. She wondered what it would be like to be Vivian, the lady of the manor. Giggling, she continued on to the sitting room. A tray draped with white linen was set near the velvet sofa. An iced bottle of champagne sat ready with two champagne flutes. Chocolate covered strawberries along with imported chocolates were arranged artfully. The heavy red velvet drapes were drawn, and the room was dimly lighted. The Victrola played her favorite symphony just like always. The mahogany floors were gleaming and covered with a Turkish rug featuring a field of red poppies. On the coffee table were two dozen long stem roses in an heirloom crystal vase that probably cost more than she'd make in her lifetime.

She sat on the velvet sofa after pouring a generous glass of champagne. Before she'd finished the glass, she heard a key turning in the heavy door and heard the sound of his heavy footsteps. He was a large man, well over six feet and burly. She enjoyed her time with him, and he knew it. He was arrogant but also caring.

He bent over and kissed her chastely.

Not what she was expecting. She sensed something was going on.

He loosened his tie and grabbed the champagne she'd poured for him. After a few sips, the crystal flute was empty. The next thing she knew he was lying on the sofa on his back and he'd pulled her on top of him. He settled her hips over his hardening shaft.

She felt her own arousal taking hold as her cheeks flushed. She leaned over him, causing her full breasts to strain against the opulent black lace of her dress and threaten to spill over their delicate restraint. She ground her hips into his as a familiar dampness permeated her undergarments. His eyes bore into hers, studying her perfect face instead of ripping her clothes off as usual.

"Is everything ok?" she asked. Her eyes still smiling.

"What would it cost to make me your only gentleman caller, Imogene? A hundred or two hundred per month? I can provide you with an apartment as well. Dresses. Jewelry. Champagne."

"Sounds lovely. I suppose you'd also take me on your business trips. Buy me lingerie."

"Yes, my little tartlet. I have needs. I don't share well."

"Only if you agree to fuck me daily. I have needs as well."

"What a dirty girl. I'd expect nothing less from a professional entertainer."

His enormous hands fumbled with the satin bow that restrained her full breasts. Her body ached for him to touch her. She helped him with the bow and slid the top of her dress down, freeing her breasts. He groaned and pressed his rock-hard cock against her hips. He gripped her ass and stood up carrying her to the bedroom. She wrapped her legs around his hips as his erection became more insistent. He laid her on the bed and tied her hands to the bed posts with the silk scarves.

"Now I can have my way with you."

He hastily unbuttoned his trousers and freed his manhood. She was amazed by how large and full his cock was. It was almost too large in both girth and length. He never failed to please her and usually made her scream. She had no idea how no one ever heard their fourth-floor trysts. She watched as semen dripped from his cock. He pulled her dress up to reveal delicate undergarments and black lace garters with sultry black lace silk stockings.

He slipped her undergarments off and kissed her inner thigh. She dripped in anticipation and her body felt like it was on fire. He took his time making his way to her clitoris before stroking it gently with his index finger. He lowered his mouth over her clitoris and rimmed her vagina with his tongue. He violated her with his tongue gently preparing her for his now engorged penis. He pumped her with his tongue until she gushed and moaned with extasy. He slid two of his fingers into her vagina and pumped her slowly at first. He then began to really fuck her. She began to scream as she sprayed him, splattering his face and shirt. After she came, he let her rest for a moment as he removed his clothes.

He untied her and brought her a sip of champagne.

She sat up. Her beautiful dark hair was a disheveled mess. She took a few sips of the crisp champagne before freeing her hair from the braided bun on the top of her hair. It fell in dark heavy waves to her waist.

He leaned over her, kissing her, pushing his bulky rock-hard body onto her. He rubbed his dick against her wet vagina, teasing her. He touched the tip of his penis against her clitoris, making her moan and beg. He circled her vagina, rubbing his penis around the edge. She squeezed his ass and tried to pull him into her. He waved his finger at her and mocked her.

"No, No, No. Not yet."

He cupped her breasts and lifted her nipples into his mouth. He wrapped his lips around her breasts and suckled her nipples. She twisted her hips against his penis, begging him.

"Are you ready for me now, baby? Can you take all of me?"

"Fuck me, baby, please." She moaned in agony.

"Do you want my cum?"

"Please, baby. Give it to me. I want to taste it."

"Not today. You are mine. I'm not sharing you, and I will finish wherever I want."

He entered her slowly until he completely filled her. She felt her breath catch as pleasure so intense washed over her. It overwhelmed her in complete extasy. He pumped her slowly until she was again begging for him to let go and fuck her with abandon. The next thing she knew he was fucking her with such reckless wild abandon she thought the bed would break. Her climax was intense and wild, just like the sex. He came immediately after she did, yelling out her name and filling her body with his hot cum. He collapsed next to her, holding her hand. A few minutes went by and he was up and showering in the attached bathroom.

"I've drawn you a hot bath. Please hop in and have a soak with some champagne. I'll send my maid to clean you up and corset you back up in a fresh gown. I'll have a carriage waiting for you outside to take you back to your apartment this evening."

She rolled over and stared at him with a mischievous glint in her eye. Her chin rested on her hands, and her large breasts spilled forward. She stood up on all fours and then turned around hiking up her dress to expose her voluminous backside. She bent over on all fours with her large bare ass begging for more.

"How about one more round. A quick one. I know you can do me one more time. Come on, baby. Hop on."

Unable to resist her, the baron mounted her from behind and fucked her until she was screaming his name. He came quickly this time. He reached into the drawer of the nightstand and pulled out a large polished stone phallus.

"You are a dirty girl aren't you."

With semen still dripping from his cock he penetrated her vagina with the stone phallus until she came in a rush of wild spray. "I'm not done just yet, baby." He slipped his cock back in her vagina until he was wet and slippery with her come. "You can take me in your ass. Can't you? Maybe not all of me."

She moaned with pleasure. "Please fuck me, baby. I can take you. All of you, but fuck me hard. Make me pay for being such a dirty girl."

He carefully entered her ass. Her arousal at its peak, she begged him to fuck her harder. He had no trouble doing as he was told, and soon found himself coming in her yet again.

He made his way back to the shower as if nothing had happened at all.

Imogene lay in an exhausted heap on the silk bedding, her hair a wild mess. He left without saying he loved her. Nothing new there, *she thought.*

She walked over to the bathroom, her senses inundated with the aroma of more fresh flowers. Lavender blossoms and rose petals floated in the clawfoot tub. She slipped into the steamy water and washed away the baron from her body. A few minutes later, the maid arrived and helped her out of the tub. The maid dried her body and corseted her dress up. She put Imogene's hair back up and dusted her face with powder. The dress was a lovely rose-pink silk with matching lace.

Much to her surprise the maid also brought her a set of rose- pink diamond earrings and a matching necklace. He may not say I love you, but I still feel his love, she thought. The stones were weighty and cold around her neck and in her ears. She looked herself over in the mirror and noticed how beautifully the stones' facets caught in the dim light.

She threw on a hooded cape, slipped back down the servant's *stairway and made her way outside to the waiting carriage. Imogene began to wonder about the consequences of her carelessness.* What would it be like to have a family? To be Vivian in her castle? With her fancy dinners and dresses. *She picked up the beautiful pink stone nestled in her bosom and turned it over.* And to have her jewels? *She laughed at loud, her wistfulness replaced by cattiness. The carriage pulled up at her apartment, and she stepped out into the chilly air.*

Ada woke up, startled, in Imogene's dressing room. Panicked breaths pounded in her chest, and she sat up. Chris was sound asleep, and her cell phone read *2:00 AM.* Feeling comforted by his presence, she lay back down and snuggled deeper in her sleeping bag. She fell right back to a sound sleep only to awaken when the chimes of her cell phone alarm woke her up at five in the morning.

Chris sat up and yawned, stretching his thickly muscled arms.

Ada reached into her backpack and pulled out 2 grape energy drinks. She watched as he immediately cracked one open and downed it.

"You are a life saver. I slept like shit. This floor is . . . it's well- uh-like sleeping on the floor."

"Well worth it, though. I had a dream. It was a good one."

"Do tell."

She went over the dream with him while sipping her drink. Now they knew they had underestimated the depth of the relationship between the baron and Imogene. Chris was shocked to find out that Imogene was a Luminary. They knew Garrett and Vivian had something going on, but they had no insight on what Vivian or Garrett were feeling or thinking. Ada spoke up as she realized Garrett might have been the one who performed the act, but he didn't seem to have the anger to be behind the murder or the motivation to murder Imogene.

"It must have been Vivian. She must have had something to do with it."

"But you said that the Baron knew that Garrett was with Vivian, and he probably knew Garrett was fucking Imogene. His employee, with both of his women . . . It could have easily have been the Baron, too. If you think about it though, I guess we should start with Vivian, as Imogene was sleeping with both her husband and her lover, plus she had her husband's baby. That would make her more of a suspect than anyone for involvement. How can we contact Vivian?"

"Well, with Imogene I concentrated on her before bed then we slept here in a space she had a strong emotional attachment to. This is where her spirit manifests the strongest."

"So it makes sense that Vivian would manifest at her home? In the castle?"

"True, but not all spirits can be contacted. We need some help to get Vivian to come through."

"Let's burn the candle and open the book. Maybe it can shed some light on what can help us contact Vivian."

"We are going to the castle today for our lecture, remember? Kevin's family owns it."

Ada tapped her chin for a moment, wheels turning. "That would make Kevin a descendant of darkness. The baron carried darkness in his heart."

Chris interjected, "Or a halfling. Or a foot soldier for the Overlord."

"If the story about bloodlines is true, then he could carry

dark DNA as well as Luminary DNA. But we don't know to what extent his darkness is diluted with a Luminary."

Chris turned his cell phone back and forth in his hands. An idea came to him, lighting up his puffy eyes. "Have you ever been to a football game? Ever seen any of Kevin's family?"

"No, never. I never go to the games."

"Well, I guess we are about to become football fans. There's a home game Friday night. Something tells me these won't be your usual Friday night lights. Especially if Kevin is part of the Overlord's posse. They smiled at each other for a moment before she looked down, preoccupied with getting her shoes on. Something was bothering her. This seemed too easy. The answers came too easily. "Don't you think it's convenient we are having our lecture at the castle today? And that our first offsite lecture was at the Vogue?"

"I get it, Ada. You mean like when a tiger Mom brings her cubs a live rabbit to practice on. It still can run away. But it's also still dinner delivered to them on a platter."

"Well put. Maybe Kevin is our rabbit? Mathias is the tiger Mom. Or Dad. Tiger Dad."

Chris shook his head and stretched. "Maybe. Man, I need some real coffee and a hot shower. My whole body hurts from sleeping on that floor. Let's get this candle burning."

A few minutes after getting the candle going, they sat on the chaise lounge together and opened the book. They turned a few pages, and then on the third page, words appeared. It was the same style pen and ink and same handwriting she remembered from the first time she'd opened the book.

For some their strongest emotional connection to this plane is vanity. Infants and children also have a strong tether. Find the place where the most time was spent being vain. Find the place where the infant spent his time. If there are answers to be had, they will come to the surface in these places. Try holding that person's closely held personal possessions.

She closed the book and snuffed out the special candle.

"It's that simple?"

"It's not that farfetched. Believable for us, anyway. Off we go. Home, a shower. And then the castle. Here we come."

Chapter Sixteen: The Castle

They stood together with a gaggle of students outside the castle. At three hundred years old, she'd heard it had housed generation after generation of the railroad baron's family. She pulled her sweatshirt tighter around her shoulders. There was a chill in the air today despite the bright morning sun. She had tried to pull her hair into a ponytail and braided it in an effort to tame it. Stray coils escaped around her face and caught in the sunlight, making her take note of the explosion of red color.

Several decorative planters sat at the entrance of the castle. Bright fall flowers in orange, cream, and purple spilled over the pots. The cheeriness of the fall plants contrasted with the foreboding and heavy exterior of the castle, five stories high, with a multitude of round towers at each corner, complete with ornately carved stone corbels and the remnants of a fortified stone tower at the front gate of the grounds. Two stone gargoyles sat guarding the front doors.

As Ada surveyed the rest of the exterior, she noted that several of the corbels had griffins perched with wings unfurled. They missed being graceful and were decidedly heinous. The castle was carved from local stone quarried in Vancouver. The walls were several feet thick, and it perched above the city. The baron's family had lived in this castle for centuries, overlooking the city they'd founded and funded with their business ventures. There were endless rumors, but few had ever been substantiated, except of course for Garrett, the notorious butcher of the baron. Ada looked at Chris as he surveyed the monstrosity before them.

Shielding his eyes from the sun, he analyzed the carvings. "Is that a griffin?"

"Did you miss the gargoyles? They look like they are ready to consume some infants. After their meal of kittens."

Chris' warm baritone *tut-tutted* Ada's analogy. His voice was oddly comforting. "Shoot. All these years in Vancouver we never came to the castle. My parents never took us, even that year they had the Halloween ball. We received invitations for some reason. I begged them. My parents would not go. Now I know why. This place is beyond creepy."

One of the male students began pretending to hump one of the seven-foot tall gargoyles at the entrance. All the students erupted in laughter. On that note, Mathias walked through the crumbled stone gates, smiling as if spending a day in the creepiest place Ada had ever seen was like Christmas.

"Good morning, students!" His voice boomed over the rumbling crowd of students, quieting them.

"We will begin our off-site lecture today outside. If you will look to the East at the griffin on the corbel, you will note that its beak is closed, while the griffin on the west corbel has its mouth open."

His booming voice droned on and Ada felt her mind drifting away from the lecture as he discussed the locally mined stone. It was all information she'd already read about. She walked over to the gargoyle that had previously been humped and reached her hand out to its gaping mouth full of large teeth. She stroked its face as if she were petting a puppy, finally resting her hand under its chin. She closed her eyes, and suddenly a flood of past emotions from a variety of people who had been there came through, violently, in an undiscernible flash. She ripped her hand away from the gargoyle as if it had bitten her. Her hair jerked in the light as she stumbled backwards, attracting Mathias' attention.

"And here at the entrance, we have the gargoyles, rumored to be the guardians of the entrance of the castle. They are said to trap emotions of those who pass through the entrance. Some people, psychics and the like, can touch the stone and feel those remnants of emotion."

She held her hand, wringing it, as if that would somehow undo what had just happened. She moved back behind Chris as all the students looked to the gargoyles and began to touch them.

A particularly mouthy student started making crude jokes. "Hey Carl, when you humped that one, was she like *oh yes baby. Give it to me. In my Gargoyle hole, under my sexy spiked tail.*"

Everyone started laughing and forgot about Ada's hand wringing,

Except Mathias. He was not laughing. His brows began to furrow.

Note to self, Ada thought, her anxiety rising, *touch nothing unless I'm prepared for the outcome.* Mathias' voice once again began booming over the drone as he redirected his students back to the lecture.

"Do not touch anything. Do not touch the artifacts. "Did you hear what I said, Carl? Do not touch the artifacts. This means you." Remember, they are hundreds of years old. Some items are even older, as the baron's family collected antiques as well."

The large entry doors began to open. There stood Kevin, grinning with his characteristic arrogance, as if it was his personal castle. "Welcome, everyone. Please do come in." Kevin made a weird sweeping gesture that should have appeared chivalrous, but only looked creepy.

Ada lowered her voice to a whisper, and Chris leaned his hulking frame down to her. "So he *is* part of the family. He acts like he owns the place."

"Explains his band of gold-digging groupies. It's not just

the NFL interest. If he breaks out a crown like a King, I am going to laugh my ass off."

The students shuffled through the enormous doors. A buzz began regarding how grand the front hall was, roughly the size of a gymnasium with ornately carved stone work flanking both sides. As large and grand as it was, it was also dark and a bit dank. New modern lighting had been installed, but it just didn't penetrate the cavernous interior.

They made their way to the ball room at the end of the grand hall. Mathias' droning voice disappeared into the background. She couldn't help but notice everything looked the same as her dream. The flooring was the same intricate inlaid marble pattern. The ceiling was a series of arches that spanned the length of the ballroom adorned with plaster rosettes. The top of the arches reached five stories and featured a series of circular stained-glass windows. They allowed just enough light into the ballroom to break up the heaviness of the castle. The lightness of the ballroom was in stark contrast to the exterior and grand hall.

She looked around to her right to see the small servant's door that Imogene had followed Vivian and Garrett through. At some point they would have to slip away from the lecture to get to the room where their trysts happened. They continued on with the tour and went through an enormous commercial kitchen on the backside of the ballroom. It featured notable amounts of natural light from a bank of windows on the far side of the castle. The windows were taller than Chris and Ada, recessed in the stone several feet, making them large enough to actually sit inside. The kitchen was fully upgraded to today's standard featuring state of the art appliances. *There must still be events here. I wonder if anyone still lives here?*

The first-floor portion of the castle to the left of the ballroom and grand hall were currently being utilized as a museum. There were a number of period items. Furniture, books, clothing and a large room with glass encased jewels.

The group trooped through the museum and listened to Mathias' ghost stories about the castle. Ada was stunned to see how good the condition was of the historical pieces. In the study a mint-condition Victrola sat untouched by time. Kevin walked over and gave the handle a few turns, and it began to play the creepiest music that Ada had ever heard. She felt like it would be burned in her mind for eternity. Mathias' voice finally came into focus for her again.

"Kevin's family has been kind enough to grant our class access to their jewel case. As you are aware, this room is off limits to the public ordinarily. I'd like to thank Kevin for his generosity."

Finally they made it to the anterior room of the jewelry vault with the period jewels. Kevin placed his hand on a screen next to the door and leaned his face up to a small red circle on the screen.

The security device scanned his eye before welcoming *Kevin* in its creepy female computer voice. One set of solid steel doors slid open to reveal a small chamber and another set of doors. The second set of doors was secured by a simple series of numbers that Kevin entered into a keypad, after viewing a keyfob that he pulled from his pocket. The creepy female voice welcomed him again and the door opened.

Ada could now see into the jewelry vault, and it was a stunning sight to behold. There were cases recessed into a stone interior wall with bulletproof glass on the front of the case. It was an interior room deep within the castle walls with a double door steel locking system. There was no visible ventilation system and no second way out of the room. One way in, and one way out. Cameras were everywhere before the room and inside the room. It was literally secured like the gold bullion at Fort Knox.

The lights were extremely bright, and they caught every facet of the jewel collection. Diamond tiaras and ornate necklaces filled the case, along with rings and earrings of every color gem imaginable. The students filed into the room two or three at a time to view them. As Ada made her way into the room with Chris, she was awestruck by the opulence of the jewels. It was clear to her now that the baron's family was literally a version of Canadian royalty. *No wonder Imogene was attracted to the baron.*

Something pink caught her eye. There in the corner of the case were the earrings and necklace that the baron had given Imogene the day he asked her for exclusivity. They paled in comparison to the rest of the jewels in the case, although the set was still quite stunning. At that moment, Ada realized that the railroad baron had only given Imogene a trinket she would consider one of his most valuable possessions, but he clearly did not. The mauve pink set was nowhere near as beautiful or extravagant as the rest of the jewels in the case. In fact, it was the least valuable item presented. She whispered to Chris and pointed to the pink set in the corner.

"That was the necklace in the dream. It's like a child's play toy compared to the rest. He was just messing with her head."

"I'm no jewelry connoisseur, Ada, but it looks like a trinket from a dime store compared to those huge diamond sets."

"Vivian was wearing a light blue topaz set at the ball. I looked, but it isn't in there."

"Well, it doesn't matter anyway since you can't touch them. That's what the book said, right? To hold an item the spirit held dear to channel them if they are to be reached."

The next set of students shuffled through the room and Ada and Chris were forced out. She looked at Chris and shrugged her shoulders. So far, their plan was not working. She whispered under her breath. "Maybe we will see something else. Maybe the servant's quarters where the tryst was?"

"It's all we have. No way we are getting in this room to handle jewels in private."

The students congregated in the hallway, waiting as

everyone finished in the jewelry room. Ada looked around the room. Her classmates had their heads buried in their phones and devices. A few were actually taking notes.

Kevin finally emerged from the antechamber before the jewel room. The security thanked him in her weird electronic voice as he exited. Kevin stood before everyone with his chest literally puffing with pride. *He's so vain,* she thought. On cue, Kevin's voice boomed over the crowd.

"Everyone. I have a special treat for you all today. We rarely open the baron's suite on the second floor to the public. However, today we will be allowing Mathias' class a tour."

Mathias looked visibly pleased. His voice, however, contained an edginess that surprised Ada. She was starting to catch on that meant Mathias knew something was up.

"Wonderful, Kevin. What a peach you are. Students, let's give Kevin a round of applause!" He emphasized the end of the sentence oddly.

To Ada's ears, the Luminary master sounded like a catty southern debutante who was thinking of fileting someone with cutting sarcasm. The students applauded on command, then followed Kevin down the hall and up the main staircase to the second floor. An artfully carved banister flanked both sides of the stairs. Each side was carved from a single piece of mahogany. It exuded decadence, just as the jewelry room did. She and Chris made sure not to touch the railing, as it was sure to hold emotions of those who had passed through the castle.

The next floor was as opulent as the rest. You could tell it was the baron's floor. There were cases of ornate Waterford crystal recessed in the stone walls. Life-sized oil paintings graced one entire hall, and grottos with busts of family members lined the other wall. Each bust had a small brass plaque below it listing the family member's name and a few things about them. The students took their time in the hall looking over all the busts and artwork. They chatted amongst themselves.

Then Ada heard the female voice of the security system welcoming Kevin. She heard the unmistakable sound of bolts sliding open. She looked towards the end of the hall and saw Kevin waving the students down to the baron and Vivian's suite. They gathered at the end of the hall and waited in anticipation. Kevin cleared his throat, appearing uncharacteristically anxious about being the center of attention. He began to speak.

"Everyone, we have a special treat today. We have a new exhibit that we've been preparing. We will be able to view the Lady of Craigdarroch's dressing room, but full disclosure — it is still under construction but will be open to the general public soon. You are actually the first to see it. Courtesy of my father, Asad, and my Uncle Byron, we will also have a dinner here in the grand ballroom this Saturday. In honor of Halloween next week, there will be a dress requirement of period clothing."

The students began mumbling, some excited and some pondering where they would attain period clothing.

Ada realized they indeed had a point. As fun as it sounded, where would they get so many period items? Kevin immediately addressed the crowd.

"We have brought in a large collection of period reproduction ballgowns and suits from a movie set in California. My Uncle Byron has a business interest in the production company, and they were happy to share. We will have the small gathering room open on Saturday morning and staff ready to assist you with finding that perfect gown."

"Students, what a wonderful treat. So very in the spirit of our coursework as well. Please be sure and express your gratitude to Kevin and thank him." Mathias had a pasted smile on his face that appeared forced.

To Ada's ears he sounded wary instead of thrilled about the treat. Kevin was oblivious, fortunately, as were the rest of the students.

Chris turned to her, his concern showing in his soulful eyes.

Ada didn't feel his concern. Instead she felt a giddy excitement about spreading her wings at Craigdarroch.

The students slowly shuffled into the main sitting room of the baron's suite. Ada and Chris decided to go last. It was vast, larger than many people's entire homes. Stunning inlayed mahogany floors were edged with a scrolling filigree patterns in a lighter wood. Unable to resist, Ada reached down and touched the inlay. A quick burst of laughter came to her, along with the sound and image of a young and vibrant Vivian. Kevin's voice interrupted her daydream before it could truly get off the ground. Sighing, she stood up.

"That's maple, the inlay. It took weeks to complete. Several of the larger suites have the inlay. The tools and pattern used to make the inlay were actually found intact in the barn. Rumor has it, Vivian — the baron's wife — once branded one of the baron's mistresse's backsides with the metal plate for the pattern. She allegedly threw it in the fire to heat it up and had her servant girl tie up the mistress. Right here in this suite. Vivian had found the mistress asleep in this very bed after Vivian returned from one of her trips to Europe. She'd arrived a few days early."

"Wow. What a lovely family story, Kevin." Ada made a point to smile very directly at Kevin as she spoke to him. *Don't give yourself away, crazy train. You have to look normal. Play it cool.* The students began to joke and mumble among themselves.

Relief flooded through her body. She turned and looked at Chris. *So how rotten was Vivian? Was she the angry jealous wife of a husband with a wandering eye, or was she a murderous and jaded wife?* She leaned in and whispered in Chris' ear. "Guess we are about to clarify a few things." She smiled with a mischievous glint in her eye.

The class looked at the fireplace and then to the oversized four poster bed. Kevin walked over to the fireplace and ran his hand over the rack of pokers for stoking the fire. The fireplace itself was large enough to fit a linebacker. It was flanked on each side with stunning carved stone. Not one but two griffins stood on either side and held up an ornately carved mahogany mantle with their talons. Their wings unfurled to reveal a three-foot wingspan. Their gruesome and squirming bodies appeared to be climbing out of the fireplace. Their faces were turned to face the room, with their gaping beaks wide, wolfishly large teeth polished and glinting in the morning sun.

One of the ladies from Kevin's harem reached out and ran her manicured hand over the griffin, before cupping its lower jaw. She bent over provocatively, exposing the curve of her bottom under her excessively short jean skirt. She began to baby talk the griffin.

"Poor ugly, wittle guy. Bet you've seen a lot of dirty deeds, haven't you. Bet you could teach us all a few things."

She stood back up and pulled the back of her skirt down, arching her back in the process as her full breasts strained against the fabric of her too small top. She smiled over her shoulder at Kevin and winked. When she winked, Ada got a better view of her, and realized the dark-haired tease was Dana.

Not to be outdone, Kari walked over and swatted Dana's ass. Every male in the room with a pulse seemed to perk up as a surge of young male hormones flooded through the crowd. "What a naughty girl you are, Dana. Talking so dirty about the griffin. I bet you could teach everyone in the room a thing or two, including the griffin."

Kari sat down on the baron's bed and crossed her legs. As

Kevin's eyes surveyed the blonde, she uncrossed her legs and crossed them again. She was wearing the exact same jean skirt as Dana, and Kevin's jaw dropped as most of the group saw that she was not wearing panties. Her pink and freshly shaved mound caught his eye and he did a double take. To Ada's virgin eyes, he appeared both aroused and surprised at Kari's audacity. Kari's blue eyes twinkled with satisfaction. She had indeed outdone Dana.

Mathias moved the class on to the next room. It was Vivian's dressing room. A decadent cream-colored velvet sofa sat near the large bank of windows. A huge mirror and dressing table sat in front of the window with an enormous wing-backed chair. A period sterling silver hairbrush set sat on a on the dressing table that matched the chair, along with various bottles of period skin potions as well as perfumes and makeup. An ornate mahogany box with a number of large drawers were open, displaying hundreds of ornately filigreed hair clips. Mother of pearl, ivory, gold, and silver spilled from the box. As Ada's gaze moved around the room, she stopped cold as a piece of pale blue satin caught her eye.

A life size wax recreation of Vivian stood in the corner on a pedestal. She was wearing the blue dress from the dream, as well as the earrings and necklace. The wax doll was so life-like, it startled her, and Chris grabbed her elbow to steady her.

"It's her," she said under her breath.

"I figured as much. She's exactly as you described her. Right down to the jewels."

A half-finished glass case enclosed a portion of the wax figure but wasn't completed.

"As you can see, we are in the midst of preparing this exhibit for public viewing later. The skilled tradesman with the security company quit in the middle of the project after he said one of the brushes on the dressing table flew at him from the other side of the room. He needed several stitches. My parents chalked it up to a possible fall or head injury on his part, basically told him he was crazy. Now we can't get anyone to come back to finish the job."

Mathias took this opportunity as a teaching moment for the students regarding demonic hauntings and physical manifestations. The students were rapt with interest, and Ada couldn't help but touch the elegant hairbrush as everyone stared ahead at Mathias.

A quick vision of Vivian sitting at the dressing table came to her. She was brushing her beautiful long blonde hair. The baron stood behind her with his large hands on her shoulders. He was talking, and Vivian was smiling, but Ada wasn't able to get much else from the dream before she was nudged back to reality by Chris. She was only able to confirm that these were Vivian's things and not props. This was indeed her dressing room.

Soon the tour was over, and Ada felt hungry to see more. They'd never gone to the fourth floor or into the room that was Garrett's. She and Chris discussed it quietly as they walked back towards the car.

"Well, we have the ball on Saturday, Chris. mMaybe there will be an opportunity to slip away. We have to be careful, though — seems like the entire castle is loaded with paranormal activity and bad energy. Good energy as well, but just so many spirits and so many things have happened here. So many emotionally charged things have gone down."

"Ada, according to our class and to some of the books I've read, some of the images you are getting are more like recordings embedded indelibly on the fabric of time by some intense personalities. Other things you might be feeling are actual spirits. So the physical manifestations like the thrown brush would represent a spirit."

"It's kind of a mix, I think. Both. It's both more scary than the Boho Luna haunting and less ominous at the same time."

"I agree. Whatever is going on at Boho Luna is much more concerning."

"So Craigdarroch is still a good place for us to cut our teeth. So to speak."

Mathias walked up behind them and interrupted them.

"Don't underestimate the depth of the horridness of the living involved with Craigdarroch. In my experience, the living do most of the Overlord's heavy lifting. The issue at Boho Luna is indeed strange. It's scary. But it hasn't currently encumbered the living. In fact, I've had a weird feeling about Kevin ever since I met him and his mother when he was three. But that is a long story for another day."

"Thank you for explaining, Mathias. We are just trying to make heads or tails of all this at this point."

"My dear girl, you are doing more than you know."

With that he smiled and disappeared around the corner as quickly as he'd appeared. She looked at Chris and shrugged. "I thought we were making progress and took the softball challenge."

"I guess it's hardly the softball challenge, but we are both learning. So when you were touching Vivian's brush I had this weird feeling. Like a weird protective feeling, and then I felt this bizarre humming ripple through my body. It stopped when I nudged you and you let go of the brush. That's totally new."

"So as we expose ourselves to bad energies we learn more? More powers just pop out? So to speak? Like some kind of weird gameshow, where each door we open has a less attractive prize than the last one?"

A raucous laugh escaped Chris. "Girl, gotta love your sense of humor. It's like *surprise*, the jelly of the week is behind door number two. Congratulations. Use that jelly jar to slay an evil murderer. Before he murders you. And your friend. At any moment."

She raised her eyebrows in mock contempt. "Hey, you could easily take someone out with a jelly jar."

"Jesus, girl, we sound like murder mystery actors on the dinner train down the street."

"Oh man, Chris, don't go there. Mathias will have us on that train next week. Learning. As it crashes off a cliff."

"So we are sort of at an impasse until we get back into the castle. I think some more reading is in order."

"True. Remember the football game on Friday. Maybe we will see Kevin's Dad and Uncle there. According to Michael, they are a real treat."

Chapter Seventeen: Illumination

Ada and Chris sat huddled together on the bleachers at the game Friday night. They both held steaming hot foam cups of apple cider spiked with cinnamon whisky, which Chris had snuck into the stadium. From their vantage point in the cheap seats, they had an unobstructed view of Kevin's bizarre little family below in the pricey boxes. There were two tall remarkably handsome middle-aged men wearing expensive workout pants, expensive gym shoes and matching Thunderbird thermal sweatshirts. They were both buff and appeared as vain as Kevin. Like father like son. Ada watched with amusement as a very inebriated uncle — or was it his father? — slapped their box suite attendant on the ass after she brought him a beer. He slapped her ass so hard the other beer spilled on her tray. She bent over none too eloquently to pick up the spilled bottle, and both brothers followed her round ass with their eyes as she bent to pick it up.

Chris started laughing. It was comical — like watching two older versions of meathead. A woman with a crazy halo of curly dark hair and dark eyes joined the men in the box. She made a marked effort to avoid sitting near the brothers. After picking a spot as far away as possible, she sat down in a visible huff. She appeared to be middle-aged. She was not virile and athletic, but more the doughy sort, with dark circles and lips wrinkled from years of smoking. Ada could see even from her vantage point that her dark red lipstick was weeping in the numerous wrinkles around her mouth. She sat with her lips perpetually pursed until the attendant came over to her with a drink and fried pickles. She knocked the drink back and avoided the snacks, flagging the attendant down again for another.

"Want to take bets on how many she drinks?" Chris smiled at her deviously and sipped his own spiked cider.

"Wow, with those cranky lips, no way. She is either a total hardcore drinker, or a teetotaler. I mean geez, look at that pucker. It's more like a sphincter. No happy crow's feet, just scowl lines. No laugh lines. That one is a pill. Not to be one of those judgey women judging other women. I'm just saying. She's pretty ugly."

"Look at that hair. Ada, it's literally like a bird's nest. That's the hair of a hardcore alcoholic who has lost interest in personal hygiene."

"If your only child is Kevin and you have an ex to deal with like one of those two ass clowns down there, I bet you'd lose interest in personal hygiene. No alcohol dependency required."

"Ok, so if she drinks more than five drinks you will be the DD home. If she stops at five I'm going to be the DD. Let's hope for less than five. I've got to keep up my cocoa glow for the ball tomorrow, and my girlish figure." Chris made a theatrical effort to suck in his gut and puff out his chest.

Ada watched the soap opera play out below. Her breath hung in the air as the night grew cooler. She pulled her parka closer around her and slipped on a pair of matching knit gloves. When Kevin's mom got to her fourth round, she gestured to the attendant and said something inaudible from where she and Chris sat. The attendant returned with an unopened bottle of premium bourbon, which she uncorked and left on the tray next to Kevin's mom. After the attendant turned, around the woman unabashedly filled her glass to the top and knocked it back.

"So much for a good mommy watching her star college

quarterback son with rapt attention. Guess who's the DD now."

Chris ribbed her good-naturedly.

"Who do you think is going to make sure she gets home after she passes out?"

"I bet not Kevin, or his Dad, or his uncle. I bet they leave her there thrown to the wolves."

"Did you see how the attendant automatically brought her a drink in the beginning? She knows her. I bet the attendant takes her home. After every game. So sad."

All of a sudden the fans yelled out and the stadium erupted in angry fans and cursing. Over the uproar of yelling and fans standing in their seats, Ada watched as one of the brothers in the box angrily sloshed his beer over the side of the box onto the fans below. He made no effort to apologize as the people below wiped the froth from his beer from their heads and clothing. Kevin's mom appeared to be nodding off, oblivious to the riotous crowd around the box.

Ada focused on the game and watched as Kevin missed the football. A player from his own team caught it and ran like a pro with the ball to make a touchdown. Kevin was sacked as soon as he missed the ball by an enormous linebacker. He walked angrily to the sidelines cussing and threw his helmet at the bench. He got in his coach's face and pointed angrily at one of his teammates, who was celebrating with the others. The brothers in the box were both standing at the railing leaning, jumping, screaming, yelling, and spilling their beer. Their tantrum made Kevin's helmet toss look like child's play. The game continued on, despite Kevin's indignant anger.

As the game wrapped up and the guests filed out of the stadium, the brothers disappeared, leaving Kevin's mother in the box. She was now totally passed out, half in her chair and half on the small table where her bourbon bottle had been placed. The attendant had long since taken her bottle of bourbon away. Ada watched to see what became of the lady with the sad eyes and bird's nest hair. Finally not one, but two attendants, as well as a young man that appeared to be her driver, came and attempted to get her on her feet. After a few stumbles the trio disappeared from view with Kevin's totally wasted mother.

Ada turned to look at Chris. She yawned, eager to get home and to bed before tomorrow's big day.

"Well that's that. It was interesting watching Kevin's family. I can't wait until tomorrow."

Chris shrugged his shoulders and looked away, breaking her gaze. He stared off in the distance.

"I'm excited, but also I sense something dark. Dangerous. If Mathias is correct, which we are to assume he is, the living are more dangerous than the dead. That would imply we need to be cautious about who?"

"I'm not sure yet on that. Maybe Kevin. He doesn't give off a totally dark vibe for me, though. He's dirty and rotten for sure, to the core, but it seemed like Mathias was referring to something more ominous. I guess we are going to find out." She shoved him playfully. "You, Mr. Cinnamon whisky, need to get to bed. For your beauty rest. So you can bring your A game tomorrow."

They slipped out of the now empty stadium and Ada drove Chris home. After she dropped him off, she headed home to Mr. Jiggles. True to form, he demanded a snack once she entered the apartment. She poured herself a glass of wine and fell asleep after her second sip.

She woke up the next morning with no dreams to remember. She focused for a few moments on Vivian, Eugene, Imogene, Garrett, and the baron. She had swiped a small silver powder poof when they were in Vivian's room and dropped it in her sweatshirt inconspicuously. She held it in her hands and turned it over while focusing. The item itself held no emotional energy from its owner, but she hoped it would still help her in her nightly dreams.

She took her time with her morning routine. She made a strong cup of coffee, then showered. She dressed in a simple yoga outfit with a sweatshirt and gym shoes. She dried her hair and brushed it carefully. A little argon oil tamed her coppery coils. She applied a loose dusting of powder over her face and some lip gloss.

Then she heard a knock on the door and found Chris there with a pumpkin spice latte, ready to drive her to the castle for the costume fitting. She grabbed her antique bronze hair clip adorned with glittering topaz stones so she could pull her riotous pile of hair up later. She made sure she packed the candle and The Undead tome, too, just in case.

The day was crisp and clean, with not a cloud in the sky. They joked on their way to Craigdarroch for the fitting. She silently wondered if they had costumes that would fit them. Chris was extremely tall and built like the proverbial brick shit-house. She was built like nothing found in nature. Women paid vast amounts of money to have the body that she had, long legs, an ample rump, tiny waist, and an overly full bust.

They pulled up at the castle, where a number of other students were already congregating outside and in the main hall. They were chattering amongst themselves with giddy excitement. Ada wished she could share in their innocent excitement about the ball. Before she could let her anxiety really sink in, it was her turn.

She walked into the smaller ballroom, where racks and racks of replicated period dresses and suits were hung. On the opposite side of the room, another row of mirrors and jewelry were on display. A makeshift row of dressing rooms made of canvas had been erected in one corner. A woman with short spiked rainbow-hued hair directed a team of Hollywood set prop workers. They hurried around assisting students into their clothing and accessorizing. Several hairdressers worked on styles that were customary during the time-period. A young Asian woman approached her with a measuring tape hanging around her neck. She looked Ada up and down and grinned slyly from ear to ear.

"Wow, Kevin's dad went all out."

"Indeed. I'm Sue, and this is Greg, your personal stylists for the event. This way, please, I have the perfect fall dress for that red hair."

Ada was ushered off and soon she was standing on a pedestal in front of a bank of mirrors. Sue and the young man measured her and remeasured her. Then they began arguing as Greg dramatically rolled his eyes.

"There's no way we can get her in the chocolate satin dress. Too much of her, too little dress." He shook his head and tut-tut-tutted.

"Well let's see. If we can't lace her up, we can't."

"The hunter green satin dress is the only one that will fit her and not compete with her hair or eyes."

Sure enough, after lots of sucking in, the warm hued brown dress proved to be too uncomfortable to wear. Her breasts were pouring out of the lacy top like a turn of the century hooker's. She looked cynically at Sue and shook her head.

"I told you. Too much girl, too little dress." Greg disappeared and came back with billowing puffs of emerald satin. They undressed her right there on the platform in front of God and everybody else. She stood in her bra and panties in shame, her annoyance plainly displayed on her face. Greg noticed her reddening face and spoke up.

"What are you so self-conscious about girl? Not a woman in here has what you have. Every guy in here would kill to spend five minutes with you naked. Except me, of course."

They all began laughing, and even Ada cracked a smile.

She had very little understanding of how others viewed her, although that was changing.

"I guess it's no different than a bathing suit."

Soon they had her in the dress and were lacing her up.

"Suck it in, girl."

Finally they had her laced up into the dress. He slapped her on the ass before throwing his head back and laughing.

"Well, would you look at that. We just made a redheaded amazon with triple D's look classy in a corset."

"Sue, in my bag there, I have a hair clip."

Sue rifled around and then handed it to Ada. She wadded her hair up in a makeshift bun and clipped it up.

"Perfect! Go on over to the accessory section for jewelry, shoes, and a handbag. You should take up acting."

"No thanks. Too shy."

She hiked up the voluminous dress and hurried over to the accessory section. Lovely earrings with dangling shimmering crystals were selected for her, setting off her dress and eyes beautifully. Soon she was sitting in a chair getting her hair done. The stylist struggled to gain control over her thick hair. She did a reversed French braid up the back of her head, which ended in a loosely coifed bun atop her hair. Stray curly ringlets escaped the braid to frame her face. Then Sue's voice boomed from across the room, directing everyone and keeping them on task.

"Send the redhead for the last inspection please in corner two. Get the girl in the red dress over to accessories please. The girl in peach, not that jewelry please. It clashes with her hair. Move it. Move it. Move it, people!"

Ada grabbed the voluminous layers of fabric of the dress and made her way to the corner of mirrors. She stood up on the platform and Sue grabbed the hem of the under layers of the dress, then gave them a robust toss and fluff. Ada looked up at her image in the mirrors and was shocked. The woman standing before her now was not the same one who'd come in with messy hair and yoga pants. She turned a little to her left and back to the right.

The sun streaming through the windows caught in the stunning crystal costume jewelry she was wearing. The earrings hung delicately down her slender neck, offsetting the beautiful dropped-shoulder neckline of the gown. The bodice laced up the front, as well as the back. The full billowing skirts were trimmed in vintage-styled matching lace. The dress was nothing short of stunning. She felt like a princess from a fairytale. Then she heard catcalls resounding through the room. She turned her head to see Kevin's father or uncle—she wasn't sure which—standing in the corner. He was impeccably dressed, right down to his designer loafers and matching belt. She felt his gaze rove over her body like she was a piece of meat. Just then she heard Greg's distinctive voice from across the room.

"Fox in the henhouse! Ladies, there's a fox in the henhouse. Goddamn he's hot though . . . Be still my beating heart."

Everything stopped. It was so quiet, anyone could hear a pin drop. Sue rushed over to the man, grabbed him by the elbow, and led him out. "Byron, please. Come on out into the main hall with me. We are just finishing up."

Greg helped her down off the pedestal and unlaced her dress. Sue returned and helped her out of it. They bagged it up along with the accessories and matching slippers.

"Do you have a date my dear."

"A what?"

Greg shook his head.

"You know, a date."

"Oh, yes. I guess. My friend Chris. He's out in the hall. Really tall, hunky mahogany beefcake."

He clasped his hands in front of him as his eyes widened.

"I already saw him. Delicious. I know just what to put him

in. You will look stunning together."

She smiled and gathered the garment bag and slipped back out into the hallway. She immediately felt Byron's eyes on her as she approached Chris. He was lurking in the far corner of the main hall, drinking a highball with Asad, at ten o'clock in the morning. Then she heard a familiar voice behind her, it was Sue's design assistant.

"You. Come with me, you hunk of burning love. I've got just the ensemble."

He grabbed Chris' enormous hand, twirled around while holding it, making it look as if they were dancing, and then walked forward. He led Chris away still holding his hand over his shoulder. Ada laughed and watched as Chris shook his head and looked down to avoid making eye contact with the other students. If there ever was a moment that she might see a man of his complexion blush, today was the day. She pretended to be preoccupied with her phone as she tried to avoid meeting Byron's creepy roving eyes. He was still standing at the corner watching the students like some sort of stalker. Ten minutes later, Chris walked right back out of the staging area with his garment bag slung over his shoulder and Sue's assistant trailing behind him. They were no longer holding hands, however. The assistant began gushing as soon as they made it to Ada.

"Oh my sweet baby Jesus. I knew just the suit. We used it on Arnie in one of those alien movies. He's built exactly like Chris. Total beefcake, and the suit fit him to a T. It's a perfect complement to your dress. I can't wait to see you two tonight."

He disappeared in the same gushing flurry he arrived in, off to do Sue's bidding.

"Ready?"

"Let's roll. I've got some homework to do before this

evening."

The rest of the day passed uneventfully, and before she knew it, she'd finished dressing for the ball and heard Chris' knock on her door. They'd decided it would be easiest to ride together, as there was no way Ada could drive in all the billowing layers of gown.

"You're here. Come on in. Could you lace me up?"

"Sure, why not? Everyone in class thinks I'm a gay man anyway now. I was spotted *holding hands with Greg* and it's all over Instagram." He huffed dramatically. "This will ruin my game with the ladies for the rest of the school year."

"I hate to burst your bubble of woe, but I think we need to focus on not dying tonight, maybe?"

"Right. Right. Spot on."

"I am getting a super creepy vibe out of Byron, Kevin's uncle."

"Which one is Byron? They look identical to me."

"They aren't. Same cold eyes, same height, same buff body and dapper clothing. Byron has more of a GQ face while Asad looks more like a serial killer who had a makeover."

"Ohh. Yeah that really clears it up for me." He rolled his eyes.

"Stop teasing me, Chris. That's too tight. I can't breathe. How can we be stealthy if I can't catch my breath? You'll see tonight at the ball. One is way creepier than the other one."

"How's that."

"Much, much better. Ready? I'd like to get there early. So we can people watch."

"After you, milady." Chris bowed dramatically, and they made their way out of the building. She struggled with the copious amounts of loose fabric. Chris had to help her get all of the dress into the passenger seat. By the time it was all in, she could barely see out the window.

Soon they were pulling up in front of Craigdarroch, where a valet was parking cars and assisting the ladies from the cars. She scanned the front entrance and noted Byron standing near the gargoyles in matching period garb. He held the same high ball drink in his hand. His face was emotionless and empty. He looked detached while he scrolled through his phone as the guests began arriving.

Ada and Chris walked into the grand hall arm-in-arm, appearing every bit the couple. As they progressed towards the ballroom, time unexpectedly slowed for her. She felt male eyes rove over her body and settle lustfully on her hair and heard their thoughts in her mind. The mixed cacophony of the men's lust interspersed with the jealous thoughts of her female classmates. The time-slow was over after a few steps down the grand hall.

When it stopped, her gaze was locked with Byron's. He stared back at her unabashedly and failed to be intimidated by the Hollywood-perfect image she and Chris presented. He dropped his phone into his pocket.

Ada realized that if nothing else, she'd gotten his attention. He opened the door to the ballroom and ushered them inside. She felt his hand on her lower back for just a moment too long and felt the searing stare of his ice-cold blue eyes on her back as she walked into the massive room. Chris grabbed her elbow and steered her towards the far side of the room. He cleared his throat and spoke quietly in her ear.

"You ok? Time slow, too?"

"Yeah. It was short. It's like someone or something is drawing our attention to Byron. I heard everyone's thoughts and felt their emotions, but as I locked eyes with Byron it stopped."

"He is one creepy dude. His eyes are empty. Emotionless."

"I know. A descendant of who though? Of dark or of light energy? According to what we've learned so far, Imogene was one of us."

"Mathias said, though, that halflings are problematic. He could be half dark, half-light."

"Or, he could have inherited a dose of pure dark."

"Here's our table, there in the corner. See the name cards?"

They sat down for a moment and watched as more of their classmates arrived. They were adorned in their period finery and the grand ball room soon looked like something from a movie set. A photographer snapped photos with a professional grade camera. A server arrived and offered Chris and Ada champagne along with a charcuterie platter to share. They sat at their assigned table and started people watching. A string quartet began playing in a recessed area above the ballroom. It was a small stage, just large enough for a small group of musicians or a few tables.

Soon all of their classmates had arrived, and the servers began bringing salads to everyone. She scanned the room in search of Kevin and his harem. She soon found them seated near the front of the room. Kevin, Dana, Kari, Byron, Asad and the football player that had saved the game all sat together at the same table. She leaned over and whispered into Chris' ear. She realized as her full breasts spilled out when she leaned in that it probably appeared like some sort of provocative gesture towards Chris, as if she were whispering sweet nothings in his ear.

"That's really strange. That football player that saved the game and made Kevin look bad is seated at the family table. Do you know what his name is?"

"Yeah, I had chemistry with him freshman year. His name is Peter Griswold. He's a nice kid. Not super bright, but nice."

"Who are those old guys at the table next to Byron?"

"They look like geriatric football players." Chris started laughing. "Look at that one. He's like a balding hulk with a paunch the size of a keg."

"I bet they're the NFL scouts."

"That makes sense."

They watched as the attendants poured champagne for the group in the corner. The attendant made a big show out of creating a flaming Irish car bomb for Peter. He brandished the glass and made a huge show of catching the drink on fire. Peter downed the drink as soon as the flames subsided. Some of the other students began chanting two, two, two, and pounding their tables, changing the atmosphere from stuffy party to frat party in seconds. Peter seemed unable to resist a second and third drink. Soon he was so drunk he nearly fell out of his seat. She watched as Byron reached a beefy arm around him and pulled him back into his seat. The ageing linebackers at the adjacent table took this all in, without a word.

Then the main course was served, Filet Mignon with a steamed lobster tail and Mushroom risotto with oven roasted asparagus on the side. It was one of the most scrumptious dinners she had ever eaten.

The students chattered amongst themselves at their tables, while the frat party table become more and more out of control. Peter, in particular, had become so drunk he'd passed out on his plate of food. Bryon and Kevin left him face down in his steak, snoring like an ageing retiree.

As they finished the main course several, couples started dancing. Before long, majority of the students had taken to the dance floor. They collectively attempted to Waltz, after being loosened up by champagne. Ada and Chris sat back and watched. A pale blue blur of silk sashayed across her field of view along with Kevin. Upon closer inspection she realized Kari was wearing Vivian's dress—the dress from Ada's dream and the dress that was on the wax model in the Baron's suite. Stunned, she looked around and realized that everyone nearby was dancing. She leaned in to Chris and began to whisper just in case someone could still hear.

"Oh my God. It's Vivian's dress."

"It is. Oh wait. Look. Is that her jewelry too? The blue earrings and necklace?"

"It is."

"That's convenient. Now that it's not in a locked room maybe we could borrow it."

"How do you propose we borrow said item? Do you think Kevin's going to be like *here, here you go, here's a hundred thousand dollar jewelry set. Go play dress up.*"

"No, but what about a time slow. My mind stays at normal speed during a time slow. So I bet yours does too. Their minds slow. Their bodies slow. I bet our bodies can move at a normal pace."

"Since when can we totally control when we have a time slow?"

"We *can* stop them from happening now, or at least keep them from completely derailing our day."

She took a long and not very lady like swig of her champagne. She motioned for the attendant, who immediately arrived with two fresh chilled glasses. She swished the champagne around in her mouth while thinking. *Why not?*

"I have an idea. So I bet Kari, Dana and Kevin will disappear at some point for some sort of sordid group sex. We follow them. You accidentally bump into Kevin and spill your champagne. While they are looking at Kevin and you and the spilled glass, I will do a time slow and snag one of Vivian's earrings from Kari's ear. They will never notice."

"Worth a try. I could pose a question as well, so they turn to face me. Maybe act like we're lost and looking for the bathroom?"

"Sounds like we have a plan. Can we try a trial run on the time slow? Maybe with the champagne attendant. Look over there at her, she has a little magnetic name tag. Let's try our plan on her, like a guinea pig."

Chris stood up with his drink in hand. He looked pensive

but also young and bullish. "Let's do it."

They walked over to the attendant. She smiled sunnily at them both. She looked slightly stunned at Chris, in particular.

"Ma'am, my champagne tastes a bit funny."

"Oh my goodness! Here, let me get you a fresh glass."

Before she could turn around to grab a chilled glass from the drink station behind her, Chris tripped over his own feet and spilled his glass. Ada attempted to initiate the time slow scrunching her face up and focusing. When she opened her eyes, she watched the champagne from his glass hanging in mid-air. She looked at the attendant, whose eyes were focused entirely on Chris. She plucked the name tag off her uniform just as the champagne splashed both the attendant and Ada.

"Oh!" The attendant yelled out as she was drenched in ice cold champagne. Chris grabbed a towel off the bar behind her.

"I'm so sorry, I must have tripped. Here, let me get that."

"You've done enough, I think." She smiled sheepishly at him, clearly still charmed by his knock-out smile.

"I'll just run and change."

Chris turned to look at Ada. She turned her hand up discreetly, revealing the name tag, and smiled from ear to ear. They returned to their seats and watched Kevin and Kari continue their dance, still beaming with pride over their newly mastered talent. The attendant returned with fresh champagne for both Chris and Ada. She was still smiling sheepishly at Chris.

CHAPTER EIGHTEEN: MASTERY

It wasn't long before they saw Kevin sneak out a door at the far corner of the ballroom. Kari and Dana followed suit a few moments later. Chris and Ada slipped out the main ballroom entrance and took a small side hallway from the grand hall she remembered from her dream. It linked directly into the servant's wing, where Kevin and his harem had gone.

Sure enough, Ada heard the ruffle of expensive silk and giggling echo down the hall. She looked at Chris and nodded. He smiled back at her, his eyes narrowing. She knew he disliked Kevin as much as she did. There was just something off-putting about him that they couldn't put their finger on.

Then they nearly walked headlong into the trio. Feigning surprise, Chris took over just as they had planned.

"Hi Kevin, Kari, Dana. Great party. I mean, geez. The whole school is going to be talking about this for some time."

Kari piped in, eager to brag. "Oh yes, the professional photographer will have those pics up on the University website before morning."

Kevin cleared his throat. "Yeah. It looks like those NFL scouts are having a great time watching Peter. Did you see how wasted he was? What a lush."

Now is the time. I can do it. I can do it. "Speaking of drinking, I've had way too much champagne. Where is the bathroom in this place?"

"It's just . . . ."

Kevin didn't finish his sentence. Chris tripped as he took a step forward, and his glass of champagne flew towards meathead. Ada initiated a slowmo just as they'd practiced without a hitch. The girls' mouths were agape, and three sets of eyes were transfixed on Chris and the flying drink. Ada reached her hand up and plucked an earring from Kari's ear. As she lowered her hand, time started again and the drink landed squarely on Kevin.

Chris fussed over Kevin with the precision of a trained actor. "Oh no, bro. My bad, let me get you a towel."

"No worries. I'm sure those Hollywood set people have another shirt. We wanted to try out some of those props anyway, didn't we ladies?" He looked left and right at his harem, hooking an arm around their shoulders.

Ada shuddered. An image of Kevin and his harem playing dress up in the staging area passed from meathead's mind into hers. *All this guy thinks about is getting laid.* Ada spoke up, eager to part ways with the trio before they realized the earring was missing. "Chris, we better find that bathroom." She did a mock potty dance that would have rivaled any preschoolers.

"It's just down the third hall to your right. Second, no fourth door on the left." Dana sighed in annoyance. "It's the third door on the right of that hallway. Next to that creepy ass picture of that maid with the giant knockers."

"Giant knockers, got it. Can't miss that one." Chris and Ada headed down the hall, pretending to look for the bathroom. As soon as they heard giggling and sounds of the trio disappearing into one of the servant's rooms in the other hallway, they turned around and headed back towards the stairway. They made their way up to the baron's suit. To Ada's surprise, it was unlocked, and they walked right in with no one around to see them. They shut the door behind them and turned the lock on the antique brass handle.

Ada lay down on the baron's bed gripping the earring tightly in her hand. Chris sat opposite her on an antique silk-covered chair. "Here goes nothing."

She closed her eyes and focused on Vivian. A blurred image came to her of the baron holding her while she sat in a pool of her own blood in the adjacent bathroom. She felt pain in her abdomen and contractions as Vivian went through a miscarriage. Pervasive sadness and a sense of loss permeated her mind. The tile felt cold and she gripped the side of the clawfoot tub in terror as she rested her head against it. The baron left her alone, and sadness began to engulf her. Then Ada opened her eyes. "Vivian miscarried. Right here in the bathroom."

"Ok, but that doesn't explain who killed Imogene."

"Let's go to Eugene's nursery. It should be an adjoining room."

They got up and looked around the suite, until they noticed a small door on the far side of Vivian's dressing room. Chris turned the handle, and nothing happened. The door was stuck. He tried again and leaned his huge frame into the door. It burst open, and a cloud of dust puffed up into the air. She flipped a light switch on and there it was, baby Eugene's nursery, filled with an antique crib, stuffed toys, balls, blocks. A dresser stood in one corner next to a rocking chair. His dressing gown lay over the rail of the crib.

Ada sat down in the middle of the room on the patinaed wood floors. She closed her eyes. Immediately she was in Vivian's body, sitting on the floor in the same spot.

Vivian was weeping heartbroken tears and holding a pair of tiny baby shoes. Ada stood up and walked over to the crib. She grabbed the tiny dressing gown and smelled the fabric. Instead of smelling dry rotten two-hundred-year old fabric, she smelled the unmistakable aroma of a baby. A clean, fresh baby. Vivian's possessive thoughts flowed through to her. He's mine. He's finally mine! *Joy, relief, and a small amount of jealous anger accompanied the words. Ada looked down into the crib, and there was baby Eugene in just his diaper, staring contentedly up at her, unaware of the fate his mother had met.*

Ada snapped herself awake and looked to Chris. "I still can't figure it out. She has feelings of jealousy and anger towards Imogene, but I didn't get any images of her actually killing Imogene."

"Maybe we should go to the fourth floor, to the baron and Imogene's red room. Maybe being in the space would enlighten us on how the baron was feeling about Imogene."

"Good idea. Let's go."

They made their way back out to the hall and up the stairs to the fourth floor. It didn't take them long to find the red room. The floor looked exactly the same as in Ada's dream, as if this wing was untouched by time. They walked into the suite to find the same bedding, same curtains, and same chaise lounge. The same furniture, too. There was a marked dusty smell and a pervasive odor of mildew. She handed Chris Vivian's earring and lay down on the bed where so many of Imogene and the baron's encounters took place. She closed her eyes, and Imogene and the baron immediately came into focus.

She was laying naked on her side with the baron spooning her, his huge body wrapped around hers in a passionate embrace. Her body felt sticky, as if they'd already made love. The baron's erect shaft pressed against her ass, insisting on more. She felt a heaviness across her midsection that pulled her body down into the bed. The baron's warm hand caressed her round and very pregnant belly. Imogene was tired, exhausted.

Ada focused on the baron and slipped into his mind. He was aroused and very attracted to Imogene. However, she felt no love. He viewed her the same as a piece of prized livestock carrying a calf by the best bull. As he rubbed his hand over her belly, all he could think about was how wonderful his child would be, and how proud he and Vivian would be of their child.

Ada woke up and sat up straight. Chris had been dozing in the chair next to the bed. Her sudden movement startled him awake.

"What is it?"

"The Baron didn't feel any love for Imogene. He viewed her like a piece of prized beef, just a vessel for his child. He had daydreams while lying next to Imogene of being proud of his child, who would be raised by Vivian. He had no tender thoughts about Imogene. He caressed her pregnant belly and only thought of Vivian."

"It was Vivian and the baron all along."

"Yes, I think so. But they didn't actually kill her. Remember when the baron asked Imogene for exclusivity? He wanted to knock her up for Vivian. So they could have a baby to raise as a family."

"This was before IVF. It was a way for them to raise the baron's biological child."

"They could have just paid Imogene off."

"She seems a very devout parent. Maybe she wouldn't agree."

"She also seemed to be living in a fairytale where the baron would leave his wife for her, and they'd raise their child together." Ada sat a few moments thinking. "Lets go to the Vogue with the earring. Maybe we can see what Vivian felt when Imogene was murdered.

"Right now?"

"Yep, and in these clothes. We will have to get back here and get this earring back somehow. I don't plan on going to prison."

"I bet they won't notice we are even gone."

Twenty minutes later, after texting Mathias, they met Michael at the front door of the Vogue and filled him in on the details.

"Wow, look at you two. Stunning! So you have an actual earring of Vivian's? That's crazy! Talk about luck."

Chris interjected. "It's not luck, Michael. I think all three of us have figured that out."

"Well, stay safe. You have one of those special candles of Delia's just in case, right? I'll be right here up front. Waiting."

They walked down to the theatre and sat in the front row of seats. Ada gripped the earring and focused on Vivian. "If I were Vivian and the baron watching a show, we'd be up front, right? Or maybe a box?"

"There are too many boxes. :et's try sitting up front first."

She closed her eyes, and just like before the dream came to her again.

She looked down to see a pale blond lock of hair lying coiled artfully against her bosom. The baron sat to her right and held her hand tightly, so tightly, it almost hurt. It was between acts, and the curtain was drawn. The theatre patrons were returning to their seats. Five minutes ticked by, and then ten. The curtain was drawn back and the actors began the next scene. When the lead male actor called out for Virginia — the character Imogene played — she never came. Minutes ticked by. The crowd rumbled. Fans began shouting for a refund. In the corner of her eye she saw Garrett appear on the side of the stage, near the stairs and the exit. He stood for a long minute with his gaze locked on Vivian. His stare was empty and heartless. He smiled a frigid smile at her before disappearing into the darkness. The baron urged her roughly to her feet, and they walked back to Imogene's dressing room. She lay dead on the floor, eyes staring blankly up at the ceiling. Baby Eugene lay fast asleep in his crib, unaware of his mother's passing. The baron yelled for help and Vivian picked up the baby, holding him to her breast. Hot tears fell down her cheeks, but they weren't tears of sadness, but tears of joy. She finally had him, her baby boy.

Ada lurched back to reality, nearly jumping out of her seat.

"It was all three of them. Vivian, the baron, and Garrett. Garrett was the one who actually killed Imogene, but I think the baron paid him."

"Let's go back and tell Imogene."

"Wait, let's grab Michael. After all, he is her grandson and Eugene's son."

After retrieving Michael, they congregated at Imogene's door. Ada smiled and prayed for the strength to help ease Imogene's soul.

"Here goes nothing."

She opened the door, and all three walked into her room. She switched on the lights and the lights on the dressing table. She sat down on the chaise lounge where Imogene had made love to both of the men who eventually killed her. She closed her eyes and focused on Imogene, then began to speak. "Imogene. I have news. Are you there?"

A faint whimpering was heard along with the cloying scent of perfume. "I'm here."

"It was Garrett that killed you. But he did it for Vivian and the baron. They wanted baby Eugene. Vivian couldn't have children."

Her whimpering stopped.

"They took good care of baby Eugene. He had a wonderful childhood and life. He grew up and married. He had a son, and his son had a son, and his name is Michael. He is grown now and he owns the theatre."

"I knew it. I knew Vivian had something to do with this. The way she looked at baby Eugene . . ."

"Imogene, Michael — your great grandson — is here. With me in the room. I believe you two have already met."

"How could that be. How did all that time pass? My last show was just last week . . ."

"I'm not sure how time passes when you are in limbo, Imogene. But I want you to know that baby Eugene was okay.

That he died of old age, and that your great grandson is Michael."

The faint image of a young woman materialized next to Ada only for a moment. She reached her hand out towards Michael, and he reached to touch hers. Michael began to speak to her.

"Imogene, you need to go to the light. It's time to pass over. You have no more unfinished business here. My grandfather, Eugene, was a wonderful husband and father. I miss him every day, and I want you to know he's there on the other side waiting for you in the light. Please go to him. He wants to see you."

The perfume smells faded away and the room felt markedly lighter. Ada held Michael's hand on the chaise lounge, and they cried.

Chapter Nineteen: The Dawn

A da woke to her phone buzzing. She pushed a reluctant Mr. Jiggles out of the way as she reached for it, before it could buzz itself off the bedside table. She cleared her throat and rubbed the sleep from her eyes with her free hand, then croaked out a greeting. "Hello."

"Good morning, sunshine. Don't forget today we have to run to the castle to give these costumes back. And something else, before Kevin and his harem wake up from their escapades last night and discover a missing bazillion dollar earring."

"Oh crap. What time is it?" She shot straight up in bed. Visions of prison orange jumpsuits were playing through her under-caffeinated mind.

"It's only seven thirty. Getcha ass outta bed. I'm on my way."

She threw the covers off and raced into the kitchen to brew the coffee. The events of last night started replaying in her mind as she hastily tossed some cat chow into a crystal bowl.

"Holy crap. I think this is going to be a coffee with rum kind of day." She poured a generous shot of liquor into her mug along with her favorite arabica and zipped into the bathroom. She jumped into the shower and left her hair up from the night before. She heard Mr. Jiggles slip into the bathroom voicing his complaints about the dry kibble.

"Don't judge, cat. No time for hair washing and tuna tar tar. It's not like you are going to waste away anytime soon anyway."

She threw on a t-shirt dress and some ballet flats. She'd just started brushing her teeth when she heard knocking at the door. She welcomed Chris at the door, toothbrush in hand. She gestured at the coffee pot, where Mr. Jiggles sat preening himself. She got a good look at herself in the bathroom mirror when she finished brushing her teeth and she almost choked. Her hair was everywhere. She threw a few bobby pins in and adjusted the hair clip. Satisfied she'd tamed it into being passable, she rifled around her makeup drawer for lip gloss and a little undereye concealer. She looked half dead herself, big circles ringing her eyes. She hurried back to the kitchen and poured herself another cup of coffee. Chris and Mr. Jiggles sat on the sofa having a kitty love fest in the early morning rays of sun that shone through the window.

"I hate to break up the cuddle party, but we've got to go."

"No worries. I hardly think Kevin is going to be up and at 'em first thing this morning, after all that drinking they did."

"Speaking of all that drinking I wonder how Peter is today."

Chris rubbed Mr. Jiggles full cheeks as he purred in ecstasy. Deep in thought for a moment, he finally began to speak. "He's going to wake up tomorrow morning and be minus an NFL contract and have no clue why. Drunken blackout time travel. Sad."

"So nice of Kevin's dad to make sure that all worked out just so, don't you think?"

"Yeah. Talk about two creepy dudes. They have such stony-eyed stares, right?"

"It's like they are blank. No emotion. Never seen anything like it. It's almost like they arranged the ball and everything just so they could make Peter look like some drunken mindless college student with no talent."

"It does look that way. I mean, why else would those jerks give two shits about Kevin's classmates? The party was wonderful, really fun, but why? Why dump all that time and money into this?"

"Something is fishy, for sure. Let's get up there and get this earring back on Kari. Where do you suppose they are?"

"Well they were headed down the servant's quarters wing, but if I were a betting man, I'd say Kevin and his never-ending-erection wanted to do the deed on his great-great-granddaddy's bed, like the weirdo he is."

"Oh my god, I think I might puke."

"Pour some more liquor in your coffee. I have a feeling this crazy train is just getting started."

They showed up at the castle just as the staff was arriving for the movie set costumes. They dropped off their costumes in the dressing room area and then snuck up the servant stairs in the back to the baron's suite. When they reached the floor for the baron's suite, super loud snoring echoed down the hall. Ada stifled a giggle as they tip-toed to the door. It was wide open and unlocked. She grabbed Chris' wrist just as he began to walk through the threshold. She pointed back and forth between them and attempted to send Chris a mental message for both of them to do a time slow. It didn't work, so she then gestured back and forth from him to her and mouthed the words *you and me*. He nodded his head emphatically up and down, signaling that he understood. She held her hand up with a single finger raised and signaled one, two, three. As she reached three they both closed their eyes and kicked off a dual time slow. She thought it better to have a wing man during the time slow instead of just a large frozen chocolate hunk in the doorway.

They walked into the suite to see Kevin sprawled out over the grand four poster bed buck naked with his mouth agape and stuck wide open in time. Dana was slumped on the chair next to the window still fully clothed with a riding crop in her hand. Kari lay the wrong way across the bed with her billowing skirts riding up, completely exposing the lower half of her body. One of her legs was folded and slumped off to the side, and a trail of half dried semen lay across her womanhood. She appeared red and raw, as if they had ravaged her in their drunken state. She wore the necklace and a single pale blue earring. Ada slipped the earring on her ear, then she and Chris hurried out of the room.

They hustled towards the stairway as the time slow released with their decreased concentration. Kevin's snores continued to echo down the hall and they both breathed a sigh of relief. They hurried back towards to the main entrance of the castle, eager to exit. Just as they made it to the main hall Byron popped out of the dressing room.

Startled, Ada jumped to face him, and as she did so, she stumbled. He grabbed her elbow to steady her. As soon as he touched her an image of the two of them engaged in a passionate kiss invaded her mind. She felt aroused and unable to stop his advances in the dream. It was a betrayal from her own body. As she shook herself from the vision and out of the time slow, he released her elbow. The back of his hand grazed her breast and she felt her nipple respond to his touch. A warmth spread from between her legs just as a flush spread across her cheeks. Her eyes met Byron's icy blues, and he looked away from her, embarrassed as his own cheeks flushed.

"Ada, Chris! I was looking for both of you."

Chris answered. "What can we do for you Byron?"

"I have an internship at one of my companies in my marketing department. I thought the two of you would be a perfect fit. You looked lovely by the way last night, Ada. Truly stunning."

He smiled at her, and she was surprised to see the smile extend all the way to his frozen eyes. It was genuine.

"Well we both need to do an internship so we can graduate." She looked to Chris, her eyes probing his.

He interjected. "Sure, that sounds great. Kevin is also in marketing, so I'm guessing you know it's a graduation requirement. I hadn't started looking yet in earnest, so this is very fortuitous, Ada. Would save us so much work in trying to find the best fit."

Chris' warm brown eyes turned to hers. It dawned on her that this was it. This was what Ahm was trying to show them all along, the god of all gods. Ahm was showing them the way. It involved Bryon and Asad, without doubt. Although she was unsure of the future, she knew deep down she should agree.

"That is very gracious, Byron. Along with the ball you threw for the students." Her cheeks flushed as her mind went back to Byron ravaging her with a hungry kiss in the vision. It was as if he had her body but not her mind. She reached out and touched his shoulder just to see if anything else happened. A vision came to her instantly of him being completely spent and slumped over in a restaurant booth, not exactly a vision of post coital bliss. There was more to this vision, and she wanted to get to the bottom of it. "That would be wonderful. Wouldn't it, Chris?"

"Sure, when do we start?"

They walked together towards the exit, Byron's voice a low hum in Ada's mind as she attempted to process the series of odd vision's surrounding her relationship with Byron. *What exactly are you up to, you rotten bastard?* The morning's early rays of sun struck her as they made it outside Craiggdarroch castle.

To be continued . . .

ABOUT THE AUTHOR

Ella Harrison is an army wife and mother of five. She holds an MBA from Xavier University and spent two decades working for Fortune 500 companies. She is an avid animal lover and enjoys volunteering at the animal shelter, the VA, and at Army posts assisting army families and soldiers. Her son, Logan, is a brain tumor survivor. A portion of the proceeds of this series will go to brain tumor research.